S.O.L.O.

ANDREW SIMMONS

CONTRACT 3

MICHAEL CLAYBOURN

DEDICATION PAGE

CONTENTS

INTRODUCTION PAGE

WE ALL WALK WITH THE shadows. Some hide it very well - behind smiles, success, and silence. Others wear theirs like a second skin, too heavy to shake off. This series is for those in the shadows. For the ones that have stood on their toes at the edge of life's cliff and didn't fall. For the ones that can't speak their truths and their feelings.

My name is Michael. I died by suicide.

But that wasn't the end.

Hell isn't always fire and brimstone. It's more than that. It's regret and reflection on a constant rinse and repeat cycle. When I got here, I made a deal with the devil. Save ten people from doing what I did, and I get a second chance at life. One soul saved, one step closer to redemption. Fail, and I stay here. Forever.

Each contract is a clock ticking down. Each person, a life on the edge, and a soul on the line.

This is Contract Three: Andrew Simmons.

A war veteran with more ghosts than memories.

Tonight will be his last night.

Chapter

ONE

ANDREW'S CELL PHONE CUTS THROUGH the thick fog of his sleep. His hand blindly reaches for it on the nightstand, the movement slow and heavy, as if he's carrying the weight of the world. He squints, barely able to open his eyes, and sees the caller ID, *Sis*. His finger swipes across the screen without thought, rejecting the call. He's not awake enough for her. Not awake enough for anything.

She'll just yell at him for something else he's forgotten. He doesn't care. Not anymore.

The phone thuds back onto the nightstand, and he sinks into the grimy pillow, pulling the blanket up over his head, but the light slips through the cracks in the basement window, too sharp, too cruel. It hits his face, igniting a burn behind his eyes. He pulls the blanket tighter, but it's no use. He's trapped, suffocating in this basement. He grabs the phone again, the glass smooth against his fingertips, and clicks it on, watching the time flash on the screen. 3:00 PM. Not that it matters. The clock doesn't care. Time doesn't care.

Andrew slumps back, lifting the half-empty glass of Admiral Nelson's and cheap Coke from the nightstand, the liquid a sticky, burnt reminder of last night's haze. *Why the hell was Izzy calling me? Did I forget something? I probably did, I can't seem to remember shit anymore.* Andrew thinks to himself. He gulps it down in one swift motion. It burns, but it's familiar. It's the only thing that's been there for him in the mess of his new life. He shakes off the taste, but the numbness it provides is fleeting.

He pulls himself upright, the ache in his back and limbs a constant reminder of how broken he's become. He stretches, but his body feels like it's been hollowed out, like it no longer belongs to him. He shuffles across the cold, concrete floor of the basement, the chill seeping into his skin. The basement smells of mildew, stale air, and that heavy scent of depression. It's the kind of place where dreams go to die.

Andrew steps into the corner of the room where the makeshift bathroom waits. The toilet is old, yellowed with age, the water in the bowl a murky yellow reminder of how little water he drinks daily. The only real liquid Andrew takes in is his least favorite, but affordable, whiskey and the generic coke he mixes with it. He takes a piss, standing there, empty, just waiting for it all to be over. Then, he turns to the sink. The faucet creaks as he twists it, the cold water running for a moment before he cups his hands, splashing the freezing water onto his face. The shock of it burns, but it doesn't make him feel alive. His eyes snap open, and he meets his reflection.

Bloodshot eyes. Scraggly beard. The scruff on his chin and the patchy, dirty blonde hair on his head only serve to remind him of how far he's fallen. He can't even remember the last time he bothered to shave. His hair is thinning, his skin pale and pockmarked, the scars on his face the only parts of him that feels real anymore.

The scars are a reminder that the man he used to be is long gone. They were given to him by the ones who wanted him dead—those people, those animals, those "towel heads" as he used to call them. They took his friends. They took his humanity. And now, they've left him here to rot.

He looks down at his camo jacket, the one with "Simmons" stitched over the chest. He used to wear it with pride. Now it's just a jacket to keep him warm. The basement is colder than the rest of the house, and that's saying something. He can feel the chill sinking into his bones. This jacket, these stains, the stench of his own sweat—this is all he has left.

You should probably shave Andy, you look gross. These scars are doing you no good. Maybe a clean shave will help you not look like a hideous monster. Plus shaving is normal, you should appear to be normal, right? He thinks to himself while running his fingertips over the scars surrounding his left eye. He traces the scars down into his scraggly beard. He only grew the beard to help mask the rest of the scars on his cheek and jaw line. He heads back to the bed. He grabs the rum bottle again, unscrewing the cap with one fluid motion, swallowing another bitter mouthful. It doesn't help. It doesn't numb the anger or the emptiness, but it's the only escape he's got left.

He looks around the room, and the walls seem to close in around him. The filth, the disorder, the stench of neglect. This basement, this prison, is all he has now. An old nightstand that's just a shelf for the empty bottles of rum and coke. An old dresser with broken handles that house very little clothes. None of them folded, just stuffed in there. He also has his bed.

A twin mattress and a twin box frame sitting on top of double stacked milk crates. The milk crates were actually functional, in case the basement floods, like it typically does. If anyone ever saw it—saw him—they'd wonder how he had sunk so low. His commanding officer would've had him doing push ups until he couldn't move anymore. His father would've been screaming at him to get his shit together. But they're both gone now, just like everything else that used to mean something.

Andy, you get your ass down there and you clean up that room. You don't come out of it until it's spotless. I raised you better than this. Cleanliness is next to godliness. His father's firm but sensitive words running through his head.

God damn it, Simmons. What in the actual fuck is this mess?!. You have 1.5 minutes to have this in tip top shape or your ass is all mine the rest of the day. You understand me, boy? His commanding officer's loud demanding voice pops in his head right after.

He stands up, the weight of his body pulling him down, dragging him to the stairs. Every step feels like it takes all of his energy. As he reaches the door to the kitchen, he can't help but think that it's the last place he wants to be. The kitchen is pristine, a picture of order and normalcy. It made him sick to his stomach these days. His mother stands at the island, a small woman with too much weight for her frame, too much life in her smile that he no longer believes in. She's preparing sandwiches, something she's always done, always hoped for, as if he would be the person he used to be. As if nothing had changed.

"Andrew, so nice of you to venture out of your dungeon," she says, her voice light, oblivious. She doesn't know. She doesn't understand.

He can barely look at her. "Hey, Mom."

She smiles, oblivious to the darkness that churns inside him. "I made you a sandwich, your favorite. Turkey, ham, Swiss, tomato, pickle, mayo, mustard." Her voice is so bright, so warm, and it burns him.

"I'm not hungry," he mutters, his voice flat, empty. That was a lie—he could hear his stomach grumble. He just didn't want to eat anything. "Just put it in the fridge. I'll eat it later."

Her smile falters, but she hides it quickly. She knows something's off. She always does. "Of course, Andy," she says, setting the sandwich aside with too much care. "By the way, Isabelle called me. She's walking home with the neighbor girl."

The words hit him like a punch in the gut. That's why Sis had called earlier. He was supposed to pick her up from school. And he had forgotten. Too drunk. Too lost in himself to even remember the most basic of responsibilities.

Andrew drops his face into his hands, a groan escaping him. "Crap, I'm sorry, Mom," he mutters. "I overslept." It's the excuse that has worked for too long now. The lie that no one believes anymore, but everyone accepts.

He inches towards the door, trying to avoid any more of this conversation.

"Everything okay, Andy? You know you can talk to me like you used to, and I wish you would," Andrew's mom says as she looks at him in that concerned way.

"I know, Mom, I know. I'm fine," Andrew says as he opens the kitchen door that leads to the back porch. He steps out onto the porch and closes the door behind him. Andrew stands there momentarily, looking at the freshly cut grass of the backyard, and looks up at the sky. It's a beautiful day. Andrew hadn't thought that in a while. He takes a deep breath and closes his eyes.

Chapter

TWO

AS SOON AS HIS EYELIDS close, he's back in the Humvee accident. Andrew and four of his closest friends, all in one Humvee, were part of a motor brigade traveling down the desert road to their next recon mission. His commanding officer, Alen, was in the driver's seat. Becky was a sitting passenger. Ramirez was behind Alen, and Danny was riding "bitch" in the middle of the back seat. Andrew was behind Becky on the passenger's side. They were all laughing and talking about the first thing they were gonna do when they got home.

Alen was going to get back to work on building that extra room for the baby that he had been working on for three years now. Becky was just ready to get the military gear off and throw on some comfy clothes and not do a damn thing. Ramirez was convinced that he was going to be a career politician after his deployment, so he had some college to finish up. Danny just couldn't wait to get back and wear his fatigues to the bar. It always went one of two ways: fucking or fighting. Danny was okay with either. Everyone was laughing and dogging on him because he wasn't very good at either. Andrew just wanted to get home. He had so many letters from his little sister and his mom. They were hands down his best friends when he wasn't around this bunch of characters.

Andrew smiled as those thoughts came into his mind. Hearing them laugh in his head made him smile. The smile quickly disappeared as the scene played through in his head. Out of nowhere, a missile pierced the front windshield and struck Danny in the center of the chest, killing him instantly.

As they were all trained to do, they reached for the door handles to tuck and roll out. Andrew was the only one that moved in time to avoid the full impact of the blast. The explosion instantly killed the other three in the Humvee. Andrew had been able to escape, with shrapnel cutting through the left side of his body and face. The scars and keloids left on his arm and ribs were easy to hide now, with his baggy clothes and military jacket. The scars left on his face are a different story. He was like the walking, talking version of Two-Face from the Batman comics.

Even after a year of physical therapy and skin grafts, there wasn't a lot of change to Andrew's appearance, for the better.

The smile completely fades off his face, and a tear rolls down Andrew's cheek. *I miss you guys so much. I should still be with you,* he thinks to himself as he wipes the tear with the sleeve of his jacket. He pulls his stocking cap from his front pocket and puts it on. He pulls it down to cover his ears and cheeks but leaves enough room for his eyes, which he covers up with a pair of black sunglasses that he pulls out of his chest pocket on the jacket. He lowers his head and heads

through the backyard into the alley. The alley would take him all the way to the liquor store five blocks away. Andrew didn't have to deal with anyone on his daily trips, and he liked it that way.

Andrew made it to the liquor store and picked up another fifth of Admiral Nelson's. He had Coke at the house, so he was good on that. He pays for his rum and places the brown bag into the huge pocket of his jacket. He heads back to his house, taking the same alley journey, always looking down at the ground. Andrew once roamed the streets of his hometown with his head held high and a wide smile on his face. Ready to engage in conversation with any stranger passing by. That was Andrew then, not now.

Andrew made it back to the house. He opens the back door and steps into the kitchen. His mom is still in there, wiping down a counter that probably didn't have any crumbs on it whatsoever. It was probably muscle memory at this point. His little sister, Izzy, was sitting at the island, chomping on some carrots and playing on her phone.

"Heeeeyyyy, Andy, did you forget to do something?" Isabelle asks Andrew in her teenager tone while chomping on her carrot sarcastically.

"Yeah, I'm sorry, Izzy. It won't happen again," he replies with his head hung low. Andrew's pretty sure that statement is a promise he will be keeping. After tonight, Izzy won't have to worry about him being late or forgetting to pick her up from any event again.

Izzy rolls her eyes at him. "It's fine, Andy. Just forget about your favorite little sister. I forgive you this time." She chuckles at him.

"You're my only little sister, dork," Andrew replies with a little smirk on his face.

"Awwwee, then it must be true, I am your favorite!!" She says ecstatically. "You heard him Mom, I'm his favorite, can't take it back now." Izzy says to their mom as she looks at him with a wink.

"I heard it," their mom says as she giggles a little. Izzy looks back at Andrew.

"Sit, I wanna show you some old pics that I found. You…are…gonna…die," Izzy says as she gestures with her hand for Andrew to come sit down next to her.

"Nah, I got a lot to take care of. Plus, I'm not feeling very well," Andrew says as he rubs his belly a little to add to the lie that he has a lot to take care of and that he's not feeling well.

Izzy smacks her lips and rolls her eyes at Andrew.

"Bruh, you don't have a damn thing to do. You're just gonna go down to that dirty ass basement. Lay in that dirty ass bed. Stare at that dirty ass-ceiling and do nothing. And, you probably don't feel well 'cause of all that damn whiskey you been drinking." Izzy says to Andrew, her hands moving as fast as her mouth.

Their mother interjects. "Izabella! Watch your language! Andy, have a seat and spend some time with your sister. I'm sure you can spare a few minutes of your busy schedule. " "You two used to be so close. Such a blessing considering your age gap." She was right. They used to be so close. They were always side by side, even though there was a fifteen-year gap between the two of them. Isabella was a late-life surprise for Amanda and Charles. Charles had had a vasectomy shortly after Andrew was born. Neither one of Andrew's parents were prepared for a new baby after almost completely raising their first child. But, as the OBGYN said, weird things happen and usually for a reason. She was right, Isabella was a blessing, and watching her grow up with a big brother like Andrew was a blessing for Amanda. Charles passed away in a work accident when Izzy was barely one year old. Luckily for Amanda and the children, Charles loved his family and prepared for the event that he was no longer with them. His life insurance and 401K on top of the settlement from the accident left them with plenty of money. Amanda was able to continue her lifestyle of being a stay at home mom and just love the kids and not be away from them. Andy took on the responsibility of man of the house pretty early. He treated Izzy like his daughter as much as his little sister. Always there for her. No matter what he had going on, it was put on hold if Izzy needed something.

Andrew lifted his head just a little then rolled his eyes up the rest of the way to look at his mom. He doesn't say a word, just stares. He then rolls his eyes to the left to make eye contact with Izzy. Izzy is just staring and smiling a huge smile at Andrew, still patting on the seat next to her. Andrew blinks at her a couple of times. Then he slowly approaches the chair next to Izzy. Every part of Andrew wants to walk away from this moment. He has to purposely tell himself to shut up and sit down. This moment won't last forever.

"Fine sis, I would be absolutely excited to spend a little bit of time with you and check out these pics of yours," He says to her sarcastically and directly.

Andrew takes a seat next to her. As he scoots his chair closer to the island, Izzy scoots her chair closer to Andrew. Izzy opens up her photo album on her phone as she nudges Andrew's arm. "I knew you would listen to mom. You have to." she chuckled quietly at Andrew. Izzy and Andrew's body language was very different while sitting next to each other at the island. Izzy was like a small child again, annoying her big brother and making him do the things that she wanted to do. Snuggled up close to him, well within his personal bubble. Teenagers today don't seem to have a personal bubble anymore.

Andrew sat there quietly rubbing his hands together over and over. Squeezing his shoulders together as Izzy got more and more in his bubble. It's not that he didn't love his little sister, and he absolutely remembers how close they were when she was younger. Things are just different now. Those feelings of joy and happiness seem to trigger the feelings that won't stay away from him. He hates those feelings more than he enjoys the good feelings. His PTSD therapist has been trying to help him in the last year since he got back, to understand the difference as well as the importance of having and accepting both the bad and the good feelings.

It has not been working.

His therapist even set him up with a help group that meets every Wednesday at 6pm at the little church down the street. Cleverly named One More Day. A group of strangers that get together every week and share their little stories of how they are making it through the days. Even though those dark thoughts cloud their minds. They come up with reasons to stay alive one more day. *Fuck, that meeting is tonight. I can't miss it. It'll look too obvious.* Andrew thinks to himself.

Andrew sits next to Izzy. He doesn't really say anything unless he is asked a question. His response is short and sharp. In his head he wants to express more, but he can't. If he does, it will cause those bad thoughts to rush in. He does not want to express those feelings or display them in front of his mom or, more importantly, his little sister.

"OH MY GOD Andy, do you remember this one? I obviously don't, but look at us, just look at us. That football is bigger than my head," Izzy asks Andrew as she shows him the picture on her phone.

It was a picture of Andrew with the game-winning ball from his first home game his Junior year. Andrew was a stout young man at seventeen years old. Instead of holding the football for the photo, he's holding his little sister, who is just about two years old, and she's holding the football up in the air. Only her little body in her little dress is visible. Her arms holding up the football that is covering up her entire head. Andrew is clearly laughing in the photo while looking at her. Andrew smiles just a little bit with the corner of his mouth.

"Of course I remember. Mom told me that every time the announcer said my name, you would look at one of them and ask 'Bubby?'"

It's also the year dad died. He actually died about six months before this pic. The team made a big deal about me scoring the game winning touchdown for the victory. Most of the crowd had little signs acknowledging his passing. I'm surprised none of them were captured in this photo. He thought to himself but didn't mention it to Izzy. He knew how much it hurt him losing their dad. Luckily Izzy hadn't been hit as hard as he had. If she had only known how great of a man he was. She would be torn up forever at every thought of their dad being gone as well. One of Andrew's objectives as he had filled his dad's shoes was to ensure that Izzy never felt the loneliness he did without dad.

Izzy chuckles, "I believe it. Sucks I don't remember it though. I do remember being there at games when I was a bit older, before you graduated." Izzy continues to scroll through the images on her phone. Stopping and laughing at most of them. All the pics that Izzy was in, Andrew was right there with her. "I swear bro, you're in more of these pictures with me then mom is." Izzy laughs again.

"Well duh, dweeb. Who do you think took the pictures?" Andy says as he breaks his character and nudges her a little with his elbow. "Mom had all the pictures with her taken professionally so she could decorate these walls."

Their Mom laughs in the background as she's standing at the stove preparing spaghetti and meatballs. " You both hush, I love our wallpaper of professional pictures," she says. "It gives our house the home feeling it needs."

She was right. Even after their dad passed away, this was their home. Their safe place. The place where they could be themselves, always filled with happiness and the best memories. Pictures of Amanda and Charles were all over the walls as well. They both believed in capturing every moment in a photograph. They thought that they would both grow old and have thousands of photos to look back on to trigger a million memories. After Charles passed away, Andrew did notice that his mom started taking more pictures than she normally would. He guessed it was her way of coping and remembering their dad. But some of them were just too much, like the pic hanging on the wall of Andrew opening a truck stop bathroom door and being met face to face with a big, burly trucker as he was exiting the bathroom. Every time she looks at it, she has to talk about it. "You were so scared of that man. Just look at your face," she would say. Well, of course, he was scared. Andrew was 11, and that man was a giant.

"Will you be joining us for dinner tonight, Andy? Or will you be eating it out of the fridge at two in the morning?" Amanda asks Andy without turning around from the stove. She's pretty sure she knows the answer, but she still has to ask. It's part of being a mom. The small kitchen falls silent with the exception of the boiling water and sizzling meat sauce on the stove. They're both waiting on Andrew to answer the question. He can feel Izzy side-eyeing him, and if his mom had eyes in the back of her head, they would be staring at him as well. Andrew flips his phone over to look at the time. It's 5:33. His meeting is in about 30 minutes. *I would really rather just grab some out of the fridge to absorb some of the rum tonight. This whole family bonding thing is making me sick to my stomach as it is. I know what has to happen, and this doesn't fit the plan. But at the same time, I need to feel a little bit of normalcy one more time*, Andrew thought to himself.

"I have my meeting in a half-hour. It's usually an hour long. I'm sure you guys don't want to wait until seven tonight to eat," Andrew says, instead of speaking what he is thinking.

The room remains silent after Andrew speaks. Amanda turns around to look at Andy and Izzy. Izzy and her mom lock eyes with one another, both with stunned looks on their faces. This would be a weird treat for them. Andrew has not sat down to have dinner with them in six, seven, maybe eight months. Dinner time used to be the pinnacle of family life in the Simmons family. Every night they would all gather around the table and talk about the day. Discuss their plans for the weekend or make any plans for vacations. Even after Charles died, the three of them would continue the tradition.

"Ummm, I mean, I can wait till seven if it's okay with you, Mom," Izzy says slowly, in shock that Andrew might actually eat with them tonight.

"I think I can combine everything and put it in the oven. It should still be good and fresh at seven," Amanda says, looking at both of the kids. "I'll make sure to start the garlic bread closer to seven instead of six," she continues. Amanda and Izzy nod their heads at one another in agreement to the new dinner plans.

Izzy looks at Andrew with a bit of despair in her eyes as she asks, "Do you promise that you'll be here at seven to have dinner with us?"

After tonight, you won't have to worry about any broken promises ever again, sis, Andy thinks to himself. "I promise I'll be here as soon as the meeting is over," he tells her. "I better get ready." He tells them. "I will see you ladies a bit later," Andrew says as he stands up from the table and heads to the bathroom next to the kitchen. He enters and shuts the door. He turns on the water and splashes more water on his face. He didn't really have anything to get ready. He wasn't going to shower or shave or anything. Maybe splash on a bit of cologne so he didn't smell like a smoke-filled bar. But that's about it.

THREE

HE **TURNS OFF THE WATER** and stares into the mirror for a few minutes. His glossy eyes reflect an empty void back at him. Taking a deep breath, he exhales slowly. Grabbing the small hand towel hanging beside the sink, he dries his hands. Andrew opens the bathroom door and heads towards the back of the house, pulling out his phone. 5:47 now. Thirteen minutes to walk the two blocks and make it to the meeting.

In the kitchen, he pauses to tell his mom and sister goodbye one more time. "See you at dinner," they say in unison. The words sting—dinner feels like a lifetime away.

Andrew stepped out the back door, crossing the yard and slipping through the gate into the alley. His head hangs low, as usual, watching his feet shuffle down the path. The church is a short walk, but there's no back entrance, forcing him to cut over to the main road a block away.

Arriving at the church, he checks his phone again—ten minutes. Great. He's on time. He notices a few unfamiliar cars in the parking lot. *New people. More stories I don't care to hear*, he thinks, his stare pointing straight ahead of him.

Andrew walks up the narrow sidewalk, passing the smallest marquee board he'ds ever seen. The words "One More Day" are scrawled across it. He forces a twisted smile. *No More Days* sounds more accurate.

Pushing the door open, he walks through the church, past the empty pews and the large crucifix hanging behind the altar. He heads to the back where the meeting room is set up—metal folding chairs arranged in a circle, surrounding a space that Dr. Williams always insisted on keeping open.

Andrew spots a few familiar faces along with the new ones. He finds a seat where no one will sit next to him, dropping into the chair with a sigh. No eye contact. He counts five participants: three regulars and two newbies. By the coffee pot, Dr. Williams stands chatting with Amir and Donny.

"Welcome, everyone! Let's take our seats and get started," Dr. Williams says, his voice a little too enthusiastic, like a second-rate motivational speaker. "Amir, Donny, come on over."

Andrew keeps his eyes fixed on the floor, rubbing his hands together. *Jesus, let's just get this fucking thing over with. I should have had dinner instead of coming to this shit.*

Dr. Williams strides to the center of the circle, still brimming with fake energy. "I'm excited to see everyone here for One More Day," he says, hitting the phrase with extra emphasis, like it's a catchphrase he's trying to sell. "You've all made the choice to be here today, and that's what matters."

This again? Does anyone else notice he says the same shit every week? Andrew glances around. *I swear he's been reading from the same script since I got here.*

The doctor continues his spiel, spinning slowly in the center of the circle, trying to make eye contact with each person. "Every day we face a thousand opportunities to give up, but you're here. You chose life. You chose your loved ones. You chose to be here one more day."

Andrew clenches his jaw. *Has this guy ever thought about killing himself? Has he ever looked in the mirror and felt, like, nothing? He probably lives a perfect life—no emptiness, no shame, no thoughts about how his family would be better off without him.*

His hands start to rub together harder, an almost unconscious movement. *This is why I stopped speaking months ago. It's pointless. Everything here is generic, like a one-size-fits-all bandage.* Andrew's gaze drifts to the ground, his thoughts spiraling.

Dr. Williams is still talking, still playing up the drama with his upbeat cadence. "Tonight's topic is 'My Favorite Thing.' I hope you all brought something meaningful to share with the group." He looks around the circle. "Who wants to go first?"

No one moves. No one speaks. Everyone either stares at the floor or glances around, hoping to remain invisible.

The doctor sighs. "Come on, folks. This is important for your growth. Talking through your experiences helps you understand them, helps you heal."

Suddenly, there's a knock at the door. Dr. Williams pauses, looking confused.

"Come in," he says, a bit louder than necessary to ensure they heard him. The door slowly creaked open, and in walks a skinny young blonde, who appears to be around thirteen or fourteen, judging by her patches of acne, braces, and casual wardrobe.

"Hey, Dad, I'm so sorry, Mom sent me in here," she says, directing her words to Dr. Williams, clearly doing her best to avoid making eye contact with anyone else in the room.

Dr. Williams smiles warmly. "No, no, no worries at all, dear. Is everything okay?" he asks.

The girl steps just far enough into the room to shut the door behind her. "Yeah, everything's fine. Mom's outside. She told me to bring in your wallet—you forgot it at home," she explains, pulling the wallet from her back pocket and holding it up.

"Oh, excellent! I didn't realize I'd forgotten it. That could've made the trip to the grocery store afterward rather embarrassing," Dr. Williams chuckles. "Tell your mother thanks," he gestures for her to bring him the wallet.

Samantha remains still, her eyes widening with embarrassment. She had no intention of venturing past the door. She glanced around the room; most people were either staring at the ground or ceiling, minding their own business. A few had glanced her way.

"Samantha," Dr. Williams says gently, noticing her hesitation. She snaps back to attention, making brief eye contact with her father before slowly moving toward him, toward the center of the circle, toward the eyes of strangers she doesn't know—and didn't want to know.

Her dad was always the center of attention in the family, not her or her mom.

Samantha weaves through a few empty chairs and finally reaches her father, extending the wallet toward him. Dr. Williams takes it with a smile, but as Samantha turns to leave, he gently grabs her shoulders, pulling her back toward him.

Standing behind her, Dr. Williams keeps his hands on her shoulders, and once again, he starts to slowly rotate in his small circle. Samantha, instinctively following, slides her feet as they both turn, caught in a strange, synchronized rhythm.

"Well, while you're here, dear," Dr. Williams says, smiling at the group, "Since no one wants to go first, I'll share my favorite thing to get the ball rolling. This is my daughter, Samantha. She is my favorite thing. Once upon a time, her mother was my favorite thing." He chuckles a little. "Now, of course, her mother is still very important to me, and I love her dearly. But ever since this young lady was born, she's been my favorite thing, every single day."

Samantha forces an awkward smile as Dr. Williams continues.

"Everything I do—and don't do—is for her. Every decision I make, I think about how it will affect her life. A few years ago, I had the chance to move us to the East Coast to teach at a rather prestigious college. But I thought about how that would impact her—how she'd have to say goodbye to her friends, how she'd need to adjust to a new life. I'd be gone more, and we wouldn't get the time together we both enjoy."

He squeezes Samantha's shoulders again and kisses the top of her head. "So I made my choice. I turned down that job offer. I chose her. She is, and will always be, my favorite thing."

Dr. Williams kisses her forehead and smiles. "Thanks again for bringing my wallet, dear."

Samantha offers a small, uncomfortable smile, acknowledging his words before quickly turning and making her way back through the chairs and out the door.

Andrew's mind is reeling. *What the hell was that? Was that staged, or was it real?* Dr. Williams had never been this personal before. His responses always sounded like they came from a self-help book. Andrew wasn't buying it.

"There, the ice is broken. I shared my favorite thing with you all," Dr. Williams says, now looking around at the group. "Now it's your turn."

Still, no one speaks.

Dr. Williams turns directly toward Andrew. "Andrew, how about you? You've been here the longest. Did you bring something to share as your favorite thing?"

Andrew doesn't move. His eyes remain fixed on the floor as he rubs his hands together. *My favorite thing? What do you want, a picture of my platoon? They're all dead now, while I'm stuck here in this dumb-ass circle. How about a photo of my old man, who left, way before I was ready to say goodbye? Maybe I could show you a picture of my little sister, who deserves someone better than this mess I've become. Hell, maybe you'd like a shot of the fifty-foot extension cord I plan to use to end this suffering.*

Andrew clenches his jaw. He wants to say all of this—every bitter thought—but instead, he mumbles, "Sorry, I must've forgotten that was tonight," never lifting his gaze from the worn-out carpet.

"Very well, then. Anyone else?" Dr. Williams asks, slowly rotating, scanning the room. "Amir? Charles? Melissa? David? Ginger? Roman? Michael?"

He stands still for a moment, hoping to coax someone into speaking. But the silence stretches on.

"Folks, this program only works if *you* work it," Dr. Williams says, his voice a little firmer now. He pulls a handkerchief from his pocket, wiping his forehead and the top of his balding head.

He zeroes in on Amir, deciding to press him further. "Amir, you've been coming for a few months now. We spoke briefly about tonight while getting coffee. Why don't you share with everyone what you brought?"

Amir, a man in his early thirties wearing a military coat like Andrew's, glares at Dr. Williams. Slowly, in broken English, he begins to speak.

"I brought my pocket watch. It was my father's. It reminds me that time is not promised for everyone, but will continue even after we are gone. Every movement of the hand means someone will leave. But I will stay."

He doesn't break eye contact with Dr. Williams as he speaks.

"Very interesting, Amir. You're absolutely right. Time doesn't last forever for anyone. Every tick of that watch reminds us to make the choice to move forward. Thank you for sharing, and I'm sorry for calling you out."

Amir gives a simple nod.

"Anyone else? We're almost out of time, but I can't mark this session as complete unless at least one more person shares."

Silence hangs heavy in the room until, slowly, the new guy raises his hand to speak.

Chapter

FOUR

HE'S A MIDDLE-AGED MAN, PROBABLY** in his early forties, with shoulder-length black hair streaked with grey and a short beard to match. He's been as silent as everyone else, sitting there with his coat over his lap. Andrew doesn't recognize him at all. He's a new face that hasn't been here before.

"Yes, Michael. Everyone, welcome Michael. This is his first day with us," the doctor says, introducing him to the group. The group gives him a monotone "Hi, Michael" and then returns to their silence.

"What did you bring to share with the group today?"

The new member reaches under the coat that's resting on his lap. He clears his throat. "Please, no one panic. I promise, it's unloaded," He says.

This catches Andrew's attention, causing him to lose his staring contest with the carpet and look up at the newcomer. He watches as the new guy slowly pulls a small wooden box from beneath his coat and places it on top. He then inputs a combination and gently lifts the lid. All eyes are now on him as he glances around the group.

"Again, it's not loaded. Please don't freak out," He reassures them as he reaches into the box and carefully removes a matte black Taurus 9mm handgun by the handle, keeping his finger away from the trigger. He closes the lid and sets the gun on top of the box.

What the fuck? Did this dude really just bring a gun to a meeting for people who are contemplating ending their lives? Andrew thinks, his gaze fixed on the man who just brought a damn gun to the meeting.

The new guy takes a deep breath.

"This is my favorite thing. I love my son and daughter to death, and I loved my wife. I loved her when she was with us, and I still love her, even though she's been gone for a few years now. So, no, I don't love this gun, but it's my favorite thing. This gun was life-changing for me," heHe says, looking down at the gun, his fingertip tracing its surface.

Andrew can't understand why anyone would call a Taurus their favorite gun. It's near the bottom of the handgun hierarchy, just a step above a Hi-Point.

The stranger takes another deep breath, his voice cracking as he tries to hold back tears.

"A few weeks ago, everything hit me. How much I had failed everyone around me. How much I had let my late wife down. Hell, how much I still missed her—I think about her all the time. I never did anything important with my life. I had no legacy to leave for my kids, Gaige and Jaelyln. I wasn't a great father to them. I was good, but I wasn't great."

He wipes a small tear from his cheek.

"One night, I had too many drinks, which led to too many thoughts. I was going to end it. There was no need for me to be here anymore. I wrote a note for my son and left it on his bed. I wrote a note for my daughter and I left it on her bed in the spare room. She doesn't live with me, but she visits during the summer and Christmas breaks. He was at his friend's house that night. I took a shower and laid on the bed. I grabbed my gun from the nightstand. I released the magazine to make sure it was still loaded, even though I knew it was. Then I racked it to chamber a round. I put the barrel in my mouth and bit down on it. I closed my eyes and slowly squeezed the trigger."

He pauses to wipe his eyes and steady his breathing.

"All of a sudden, I heard someone whisper my name. My eyes snapped open just as my finger finished squeezing the trigger. Keep in mind, all of this happened in a split second. The gun clicked, but it didn't fire. A huge wave of relief washed over me, and I started crying. I couldn't figure out why it didn't fire—it had never jammed before. In that moment of relief, panic, and anger, I screamed and pointed the gun at the ceiling. I pulled the trigger again, and this time, it fired the round that was in the chamber, leaving me with a constant ringing in my ear as a reminder. That's when I realized it wasn't my time. It wasn't time to leave my children without their dad, and it wasn't time for me to leave this world."

The man wipes more tears away and picks up the Taurus again, staring at it.

"So, this is my favorite thing. It always worked perfectly, and maybe, just maybe, it worked perfectly in that moment too."

He lifts the lid of the box, places the gun back inside, and closes it.

"It still sits next to my bed, but now it stays in its case, unloaded."

Andrew sat through the new guy's whole story without looking away once. His story actually encapsulated a lot of his own feelings. *I still can't believe this guy brought a damn gun to a meeting group about suicide. Who the hell has the audacity to do that? Who the hell has the balls to do that? Either way, I'm kinda proud of him,* Andrew thought to himself, and for a moment, he felt a bit of peace come over him. The peace only lasted a few moments before the demons in him had to chime in with their two cents on the situation. *Wait a minute... he didn't make the choice not to pull the trigger. The fucking gun jammed, and then he pussed out. That's a total cop-out. He didn't make the decision. He was given a second chance to fuck everything up again,* Andrew thought, the wave of comfort leaving his body.

The small group of individuals all applauded the newcomer and thanked him for sharing his story. He nodded his head with a half-assed smile on his face as his hands rested on top of his coat, covering the gun case.

"Well, there you have it, folks," Dr. Williams said victoriously. "There can always be one more day. It's all up to you to choose that. It's up to you to look at that person staring back at you in the mirror and tell him NO!" the doctor said, raising his fist in the air. "I believe in each and every one of you here today. This is a hard thing to do. It's hard to come to terms with the fact that you are not okay, but with time and support, you can be okay." Dr. Williams paused and looked around the room for dramatic effect. "And I promise you, if you keep coming to these meetings and doing the mental exercises recommended by your therapists, you too, one day, will be okay."

The mental exercises? Those are a joke as much as this meeting is. Stand in the mirror for 10 minutes a day and tell yourself that you mean something, that you're worth something, that there is something more. I'm confident my pretty boy doctor has never had to look into a mirror, horribly scarred, and tell himself that he has something to live for, Andrew thought. In reality, Andrew did try the exercises. He tried his hardest to do them. He couldn't stomach looking at himself for that long. The scars looking back at him drowned out the fake words he was telling himself. At least when he got drunk, he could look in the mirror and laugh at his pain and reflection. On a few occasions, he attempted to give himself the pep talks while drunk. Those nights ended worse for Andrew.

"Okay, I think that's our time for tonight," the doctor said as he looked at his watch. "I hope everyone got something out of tonight's meeting, and I look forward to seeing you all next week, same time."

The group got up, put on their coats, and stretched. The doctor and a few of the participants surrounded the new guy, probably to thank him for sharing and ask him more questions.

Andrew immediately stood up and turned around to head out the door. He didn't bother to stick around for the Q&A. He only came to these meetings as a requirement and formality. He adjusted the hood of his coat to pull it over his head. He opened the door to head outside and make the walk back to his house. It was dark now, but he still put on his sunglasses. They had become more of a security blanket than practical at this point.

Chapter

FIVE

HE MADE THE WALK DOWN the street, cutting over into the alley. *I should stop and grab some alcohol. This is probably gonna be a long night,* Andrew thought. *Wait, I grabbed some earlier.* The quick thought of already having a bottle at the house made him smile. It was weird, the things that made him smile these days versus the things that used to make him smile. *Okay, get to the house. Head downstairs. Grab a couple of drinks to catch a buzz for this dinner. Brush my* *teeth to get rid of the smell before heading back up. Head up and sit through dinner. Make it seem real to Izzy and Mom. Hug them goodbye but tell them goodnight. Head downstairs. Have a few more drinks, but be quiet. Don't be loud. Wait for the sound of the TVs upstairs to go silent.*

They'll either be asleep or in their bedrooms. Have a few more drinks. Take a shower. Do what needs to be done. Andrew walked himself through how the rest of his night would go.

Andrew reached the gate door to their backyard. He opened it and walked through. His short twenty steps to the back door seemed to take forever. His mind wandered, playing out family memories in the backyard. The swing set still sat there, all rusted with little patches of faded dark green paint. It had been sitting in that same spot since Andrew was seven years old. As soon as he was too old to enjoy it, Izzy had the opportunity.

Two bare spots of ground about fifteen feet apart—that's where Andrew and his dad would play catch every single day after school before dinner. He never understood why the grass didn't grow back after all these years. For many years after Andrew's dad passed away, he believed it was his dad's way of keeping his memory alive with Andrew. Andrew believed it so much that for months after he passed, he would head outside, stand in his spot, and just toss a ball up in the air and catch it over and over again while talking to him. He would still tell him about his day, every day for months.

Izzy's little wooden house was right next to the shed on the other side. So many times they would all gather around and attempt to squeeze their adult bodies into her quaint four foot by five foot plastic house anytime she would invite them over to "her house" for snacks and soda.

In that moment, Andrew thought maybe his parents were a couple of hoarders, and he was just now realizing it.

Andrew opened the door and was greeted by Izzy's smiling face staring at him. A plate of steaming spaghetti sat on the island in front of her.

Their mom was at the stove, scooping another plate of spaghetti from the pot onto a plate. She turned around as Andrew shut the door and sat on the island in the spot next to Izzy.

"Well, look who showed up on time as he promised. It's safe to say I am shocked, but pleasantly," Andrew's mom said, looking at him with the same smile that sat on Izzy's face. It was definitely passed down in the genes.

"Hey guys, I said I would be here right after the meeting," Andrew replied, directing his comment to both of them. His tone was soft and uneasy. He couldn't believe they would think he would not be there on time. They had every reason not to believe him, though. The value of Andrew's word had greatly declined over the year he had been back home.

"Let me run downstairs and splash some water on my face. Then I'll be back up to eat," Andrew said as he walked to the basement door and opened it. He looked behind him at Izzy and his mom. "Give me five minutes, and I'll be right back up." He offered a brief, fake smile to his family as he stepped through the doorway, looking behind him before he closed it.

Andrew walked down the flight of creaky wooden steps. Each one was more creaky than the one before it. They probably should have been replaced a long time ago. Andrew's dad was a good man who made sure to take care of the house. But he still had rules he lived by. One of those was, if it's not broken, don't fix it. The stairs were made of strong wood, and they would last the lifetime of the house, he always told them—especially Andrew's mom, who had traveled up and down these stairs daily for decades, washing and drying the family's clothes.

Andrew reached the bottom of the stairs and looked at his unmade bed. He patted down his coat before he took it off. He felt the bottle of rum, still in the huge pocket on his right side. *How the hell did I forget that was in there? I should have already been sipping on this. That would have made that damn meeting a lot more bearable,* Andrew thought as he pulled the bottle out and twisted off the lid without hesitation. He tilted his head back and took two large gulps. He walked to the nightstand next to the bed and placed the bottle down. He continued to go through all the pockets, pulling out miscellaneous items that had probably been hiding in there for months. He tossed all the old receipts in the trash can next to the nightstand.

Andrew grabbed his cell phone out of his breast pocket and clicked the button to turn it on. The screen was blank with just the time: 19:21. There were no new notifications, as usual. Andrew had done pretty well at sticking to himself after he got out of physical therapy and rehab—isolating himself with his thoughts and abandoning everyone that used to mean something to him, or to whom he used to mean something.

He clicked the button to lock the screen and set it down right next to the bottle of Admiral Nelson's. He patted himself down one more time to make sure that all the pockets were empty. He removed the coat and the button-down flannel that he was wearing and walked around the bed to the other side where the old washer and dryer had been sitting in the same spot for the last decade of his life. *If it ain't broke, don't fix it.* He tossed them both in the washer, poured some detergent over the garments, and started the cycle.

He made his way back towards the bathroom, picking up the random clothes that were on the ground. No need to leave his mother a dirty room to clean up. Andrew tucked the dirty clothes under his left arm and used his right hand to reach for the bottle of rum. He twisted the top off and took a few more swigs. Setting it back down, he headed into the bathroom and tossed the armful of dirty clothes into the hamper. He approaches the sink and turns the water on, using his fingertips to test the temperature before cupping his hands and splashing the water on his face. He let the cool water drain down his face as he opened his eyes and looked in the mirror.

Andrew can already feel the buzz kicking in. He glares into the mirror and gets lost for a moment. With his shirt off and just wearing a beater, the shrapnel scars are a lot more visible—some of them deep and long, varying in color. The doctor had explained to him why some were red and purple, but he didn't really pay attention. The only thing he knew was they were scars, and they were hideous. The scars moved up his left arm and onto his neck. They resembled tiger stripes to Izzy, who had accidentally seen them once when Andrew didn't think anyone was home, and he went upstairs to grab a sandwich.

He grabs the toothbrush off the edge of the sink and runs it under the water before grabbing the toothpaste and squeezing out some onto the bristles. He brushes his teeth without looking in the mirror. He spits the toothpaste out and scoops a handful of water to swish around in his mouth. He hopes that will be good enough to get the scent of the rum off his breath.

Andrew stared at himself for one more moment before splashing more water on his face and running his wet hands through his hair. He turned off the water and grabbed a long sleeve white t-shirt off the hook by the mirror. He had placed it there a few days ago for a shower that he ended up forgetting to take. After he slipped into the shirt, he began his trip back up the stairs for his last dinner with Izzy and his mom.

Chapter

SIX

WALKING UP THE STAIRS, ANDREW thinks to himself, *This will be okay. Make sure to smile a lot. They both still love your smile. Dinner and chatting will probably only last an hour or so. Keep your shit together. Don't say stupid shit to bring them down. That doesn't need to be your last memory of them. More importantly, that doesn't need to be their last memory of you.*

Andrew pauses at the door and takes a couple of deep breaths. He puts his favorite fake smile on his face and opens the door to the kitchen for the last time.

Andrew is greeted again by Izzy and his mother. Both are now sitting down at the island. Their plates in front of them are still steaming. Mom always made sure the kids ate hot food for dinner. Izzy and Amanda are each eating a small bowl of salad. It was always the same in the house. Andrew always loved the structure. If they were having anything pasta-related, you could rest assured there would be a side salad you would have to eat before the main course. Andrew was never really a fan of the salad. He was always a growing, active boy, then man. He wanted meat and carbs, but he respected his parents and appreciated everything they did for him. He would eat the salad every time with a smile on his face.

"Oh, I'm sorry, dear," his mom says to him with her mouth full of salad and a hand covering her lips. "You took a bit longer down there than I thought you would. Hope you don't mind we started with our salads, waiting on you."

Izzy chimes in with her mouth full of salad and lips covered in her favorite ranch dressing. "I'm not sorry, I'm starving. I was about to eat your salad too." Izzy always loved the salads on pasta dinner nights. With the amount of ranch dressing she would pour all over it, Andrew was convinced she really only liked the dressing. The salad was something she had to deal with. *Who the hell likes salad anyway?*

Andrew lets his intrusive thoughts come out of his mouth instead of keeping them in. "Izzy, I'm pretty sure your salad doesn't even count as a salad anymore. Look at all that damn dressing. Mom might as well just have poured the container in a bowl and given you a spoon." Andrew musters up a small chuckle. "I dare you to eat my salad with no dressing." He points at the bowl in his spot.

Both Izzy and Amanda pause for a moment. It's the first time they've witnessed Andrew attempt to be funny in months. Izzy looks at Andrew's salad and then at Andrew. "That's absolutely disgusting, Andy. A salad without dressing? That's like just eating grass. But, you're onto something." She turns to her mom. "Next time, can I just have a bowl of dressing?"

All three of them laugh at the comment as Andrew pulls out his stool and takes a seat.

"Absolutely not, young lady. I better not catch you in here taking swigs of that ranch dressing either. Now that Andy has put that in your head," Amanda says, pointing at Izzy with her fork.

Andy grabs the ranch dressing that's sitting in front of Izzy's bowl and squeezes a bit onto his salad. He mixes it around a few times with his fork before taking his first bite. It's been a while since he's had real food. Most of his diet these days is Ramen noodles and rum. Either that or just rum for the day with an occasional snack of crackers or something to help "absorb" the alcohol.

"Oh, wait, wait. I have an idea!" Amanda says suddenly with excitement in her voice. "I know we already started eating our salads before you made it to the table. So, technically dinner had already started. But, would you two mind doing your dear mama a *huuuge* favor?"

Andrew and Izzy knew they were in for some real family-type stuff. Anytime Amanda wanted to do something they wouldn't like but would make her really happy, she'd toss in *dear mama* and *huge favor*. Izzy spoke up first.

"Sure, what's up, mama?"

Amanda pauses and smiles at both of them, bouncing her focus between their faces that have changed so much over the last dozen-plus years. She puts her hands on the island top and takes a deep breath.

"Do you kids mind if we say a prayer before we eat? Please, it would mean so much to me. We haven't said what we're thankful for in forever," she asks, almost with a pleading voice.

I don't think this is a time to pray. I think the time for praying has passed us. I would rather just eat and fake my way through this, Andrew thinks to himself. He opens his mouth, about to tell his mom that he's starving and they should just eat.

Izzy was faster to open her mouth than Andrew. Of course she was. She was a loud-mouthed teenager. "That's a great idea, Mama. Of course, we can say a prayer and what we're thankful for," she belts out as she extends one hand across the table to grab Amanda's hand. She extends the other one to Andrew. Amanda grabs her hand and extends her other one across the island towards Andrew.

What the fuck, Izzy? Speak for yourself. I don't want to do this. No part of me wants to do this, Andrew thinks to himself while quickly considering his options. He could say no thanks and ruin this dinner for them, and that would be their last memory—Andrew ruining something yet again.

Or he could suck it up, put his thoughts at bay for a moment, and just participate. Even if his participation is fake, they'll never know that.

Andrew stares blankly at his salad, not realizing they were both still holding their hands out toward him. He maintains his blank stare until he sees Izzy's fingers wiggling out of the corner of his eye. He clears his throat and apologizes before gripping Izzy's hand with his left and meeting his mother's hand in the middle of the island with his right. Andrew knows they can both feel how clammy his hands are. They've been that way for a long time now, thanks to the stranglehold of alcoholism.

Once Andrew's hands complete the circle, a wide smile forms on Amanda's face. "Great. This is nice," she says. "I guess I'll go first. It's been a while since we've done this, and I don't know when the next time will be that we get the opportunity to be together again for family dinner."

Hearing his mom say those words instantly causes pressure in Andrew's chest. He knew when the last time would be. *This time.* He instantly feels like pulling away, but he gathers enough strength to stay in the moment.

"Thank you, Lord, for this dinner you have provided us tonight," Amanda says, her head down and eyes closed. Andrew looks over at Izzy. Her head is down and eyes closed as well. He thinks for a moment whether he should close his eyes too. He doesn't like the visions he gets when he closes his eyes, so he stays focused on his mom while she finishes her prayer.

"Thank you for two wonderful kids with two completely different personalities that have kept me on my toes their entire lives. Thank you, Lord, for giving me Charles. I miss him so much every day, but I'm so thankful I see so much of him in Andrew—strong, resilient, protective."

Mom, I haven't been any of those things in a long time. I'm weak, I'm fragile, and I can't protect anything. I couldn't protect my friends in the war. I can't protect Izzy from anything. I am not the man that Dad was, Andrew says to Amanda in his thoughts. He would never say those words out loud, even though he's thought about them often.

"I get to see so much of him in Izzy as well—empathetic, caring, and adventurous. I'm thankful for the house that we have turned into a home. I'm thankful for the home they have made in my heart. Amen."

Amanda finishes her prayer, grabbing her paper towel to wipe the tears from her eyes, then wiping her nose.

Andrew hurries to lower his head and close his eyes so his mother doesn't catch him not bowing his head in prayer. She lifts her head up and squeezes both of the kids' hands.

"Izzy, would you like to go next?" she asks.

"Sure, I'll go," Izzy says. Amanda lowers her head again as Andrew raises his. He can see the tears still forming on his mother's eyelashes. He looks over at his little sister and sees the same tears forming.

"Thank you, Lord, for this food we are about to eat. I'm thankful for my family and friends. I'm thankful that Mom discovered how to work a camera when she was younger. While I never really got to know our dad, thanks to Mom's excessive picture-taking, I will never forget how amazing of a person he was." Amanda chuckled a little bit at that comment. Andrew watched as the tears on Izzy's eyelashes formed even more before one broke away and dropped to the island top where her head was bowed. He felt his chest get even tighter.

"I'm thankful that you gave me a big brother like Andy. He has always been an inspiration for me to do better, to make the right choices. He has always been there, right by my side, to help me with anything I needed, to hug me when I needed it, to be honest with me when no one else would be. To be my brother and my best friend. I pray that you help him with this slump that he has been in. I hope you show him that everything is okay. What happened in the war was not his fault, and his small family loves him greatly." Izzy leans her head over to her shoulder to wipe off another tear that is about to fall.

"I would also like to thank you, Lord, for ranch dressing. It's really good." Izzy said sarcastically. Both Izzy and Amanda laugh out loud. Izzy was always good at saying something meaningful followed by something funny or sarcastic to break the tension. She did not disappoint in her prayer.

Amanda looks up and catches Andrew with his head not bowed in prayer. He is locked in on Izzy's face. She clears her throat a few times before Andrew realizes the throat clearing is directed at him. He breaks his stare at his little sister and directs his attention to his mom. He can see the tears in her eyes, and it appeared that a few had rolled down both her cheeks.

"Would you like to go, Andy?" she asks him. Andrew pauses. Not one part of him wanted to go. If it was up to him, he would drop both their hands and head back down into his dilapidated home under this perfect house. He had already promised himself that he wouldn't let something like that be their last memory of him. He took a deep breath and replied, "Sure, Mom." Amanda bowed her head back down. Andrew bowed his head down for just a second, then looked back at his mom with her head bowed.

"Thank you, Lord, for this food we are about to eat. I'm also thankful for my father. He was strong. He was resilient. He was a protector. He was everything Mom has told Izzy he was her entire life. I wish she would have gotten a chance to meet him. She would have loved him as much as we did and do." Andrew clears his throat. Thinking about these things was not good for his mentality. They were normal thoughts, but they destroyed him on the inside. He could feel the need for more alcohol in his system right now.

"I'm thankful for our mother. When Dad died, Mom didn't hesitate to walk in his shoes and do her best to raise us the same way they would have together. She never let us feel unloved or unwanted or a burden. She sacrificed so much to be a stay-at-home mom and be there for us for anything that we needed growing up. She encouraged us to be ourselves and do all the right things in life. She let us make mistakes and learn from them. She stopped us from making life-threatening choices, which was great for me as a rebellious, overactive young man. She made sure to always share stories of Dad to keep his memory alive with us." Andrew looks over at Izzy and can see more tears on the island top. He can see her doing her best not to let out any cries, her lips tight to keep the noise in.

"I'm thankful that you gave us an amazing woman to be our mother." Andrew takes another pause and clears his throat. He can feel his eyes begging to water. He hated that feeling. He needed it to stop. He could not feel this way, not in this moment. He takes another deep breath.

"I'm thankful for my little sister, who has been my best friend for the last fourteen years. I'm thankful that she has our mom's personality and would give up the world to see one person smile. I'm thankful that she, or that we, have been a part of each other's everyday life for so long. I'm thankful that she looks up to me as an inspiration—her words, not mine." Izzy and Amanda let out a little laugh through the tears at Andrew's one-liner. "I'm thankful that the person I am today is not looked at as her person of inspiration. I hope for the rest of her life she remembers me as the person I was before the war. I hope that she always knows that she was my inspiration as well." Andrew realizes that he has started talking about himself in the past tense. He didn't want to alarm either one of them. He quickly clears his throat and ends his prayer with, "I'm also thankful for this spaghetti that is probably cold now but still delicious. Amen, let's eat."

Izzy and Amanda lift their heads up and say "Amen" as they wipe their tears from their eyes.

"Well, that was wonderful. Absolutely wonderful," Amanda says. "We have to do one more thing though." She gets up and walks around the island to their side as she picks up her phone from the island. She positions herself in between both of them. "We have to take a picture. We have to." She opens the camera on her phone. Izzy and Andrew squeeze in tighter to be in the selfie. Andrew makes sure to turn his head to the left even further to ensure that his scars are not shown. Amanda says, "On three, say cheese." She counts down and exclaims, "Cheese!" Andrew and Izzy follow along. Amanda snaps the selfie and looks at it. With a wide smile, she says, "Wonderful, absolutely wonderful."

Chapter

SEVEN

ANDREW SAT THROUGH DINNER WITH his mom and little sister. They spent their time laughing, telling jokes, and remembering the past. This is exactly how Andrew wanted to leave them—smiling and laughing, remembering him before the accident, before everything changed. Before Andrew changed.

Once they finished dinner, Izzy volunteered herself and Andrew to clean up while Amanda went into the living room to watch the rest of her shows. Izzy and Andrew gathered all the plates from the table and took them to the sink.

"Thanks, Andy. I'm really glad you didn't flake on us and immediately go down to your dungeon when you got home," Izzy said to Andrew as she placed the drainer in the sink and turned on the water.

"No worries, sis, I promised I would. I figured I might as well keep one promise before—" Andy stopped himself before finishing what he was going to say. He coughed and covered his words up. "Do you plan on putting any dish soap in there, or are we just gonna wash these in hot water?"

Izzy laughed and grabbed the dish soap. She squeezed some of the soap into the water and laughed at herself. "I mean it, Andy. I really am thankful for all those things I said. I couldn't imagine having any other brother in my life. I know when you came back with your injuries, things just kinda changed, and you weren't the same person you were when you were deployed."

Andrew handed her a stack of plates to drop into the hot, soapy water. "I really don't wanna talk about that, sis, if that's okay with you. Let's just enjoy this time," he told her.

"No, I get it. I won't talk about it. We don't have to talk about it. I just want you to know, I may just be your bratty little sister with very little real-life experience." Izzy paused to hold back another tear. "But I will always be here for you, just like you have always been there for me and mom."

I wish I could tell you that I will always be here for you too, little sis. I won't, though. I wish I could tell you that I'll always be a shoulder for you to cry on, that I'll always be a movie and popcorn night buddy. I won't, though. I wish I could tell you that I'm alright and you have nothing to be worried about. I can't, though, Andrew thought to himself.

"Aww, thanks, Izzy. That means a lot. You know, for being an annoying, bratty little sister, you're pretty cool and way ahead of your age," he told her instead.

Izzy paused from doing the dishes and abruptly turned to Andrew, wrapping her arms around him. Her soapy hands grabbed onto his shirt. "I love you," she whimpered into his chest.

"I love you too, sis," Andrew replied, gripping her in his arms as well. They embraced each other for a few moments in silence. Andrew broke away first as those feelings that tear him down started to creep inside him. He pulled out his phone to check the time. His eyes widened as he realized the time.

"Shit," Andrew said before his mom's voice came from the front room, simply telling him to watch his language. Andrew and Izzy looked at each other sarcastically and held back their laughter. It was always funny to them to hear her tell them to watch their mouths. Sometimes it would be non-vulgar words used out of context. It was okay for them to discuss Hell as a location. If they were to say "Go to Hell" or "What the hell," then they would get the "Watch your mouth" from their mom.

Andrew lowered his voice just a little bit. "Shit, I didn't realize it's almost 9:30. I gotta head downstairs and finish up laundry and get some sleep." He embraced her for one more hug and gave her a kiss on the cheek.

"Okay, whatever. Good night, bro. I'll see you tomorrow," she told him.

I hope you don't have to see me tomorrow, Andy thought to himself. "You bet," he replied. He walked around the table and peered into the living room where Amanda was sitting on her favorite chair. "Goodnight, Mom," he said across the room. She looked over at Andy as she muted the show she was watching. It had been a while since Andrew had told her goodnight.

"Goodnight, son, I love you. Don't make too much ruckus down there," she said with a smile on her face.

Andrew paused for a moment, taking in the image of his mother's smiling face one last time. "I love you too, Mom." Andrew jerked forward slightly, then stopped himself. He wanted to give her a hug, not for him, but for her. He couldn't bring himself to do it though, not in this moment.

Andrew opened the basement door and stepped down a few steps, closing the door behind him. Andrew's demeanor changed as he slowly walked down the stairs. He was fully aware of what was going to happen tonight. He was fully capable of not letting it happen, but it was going to happen. He made his way to the washer and dryer. He popped the lid of the washer open and transferred the damp clothes over to the dryer. He shut the door and turned it on.

Andrew stood there a moment, looking out the small window above the dryer at the night sky. It was beautiful. The window was covered in cobwebs on the inside. The outside of the glass had a permanent green hue to it from years of trimming the weeds and having chopped weeds thrown at it. He thought to himself how the window was a metaphor for his life. There was so much beauty around him on the outside, but it was constantly hard to see it through all the mess that could easily be cleaned up but hadn't been. Now it was too late.

Andrew turns to his bed and heads to it. He sits on the edge and pours himself a drink—a mixture of Admiral Nelson's and Coke—into an old styrofoam cup that has probably been re-used for days. He takes a few huge gulps and sets it down before laying back on the bed. He stares at the ceiling, doing his best to clear his mind. He had no such luck. No matter how much he drinks or how many prescribed pills he takes, the memories don't go away. They replay again and again, just as they have since he returned home. No matter what good has happened or what support he's had, those memories are still there, suffocating every thought he has about belonging.

He turns on his side, grabs the cup, and takes another large gulp. He pulls out his phone. It's 10 o'clock.

Mom will be out cold in a half hour. An hour, at most. Izzy will probably be up for a while, even though she has school tomorrow. I don't know why Mom doesn't go into her room and shut off her lights at 10 p.m. like she always used to do to me. I need to finish up the clothes and probably take a shower. I should probably shower now so I don't forget, Andrew thinks to himself.

EIGHT

ANDREW SITS UP IN BED and stands. A little stumble hits him, and he braces himself by putting a hand on the wall. He gathers his balance before grabbing the big gulp cup and chugging the rest of the rum and Coke. He places the empty cup on the nightstand and walks to his dresser to grab a pair of boxers and a beater. He'll put on fresh jeans and a shirt when the dryer is done. He heads to the bathroom and turns on the shower. Once the water temperature feels right on his hand, he takes off his clothes and steps in. It's a modified shower out of an old RV that was just placed there and fabricated in a hurry. It didn't even have a shower door. They made it work by placing a clothesline inside and hooking a regular shower curtain to it.

Andrew stands in the shower with his hands against the wall, letting the water run down his head and over his body. He was never the type to cry openly. He kept his emotions to himself for the most part. Even in the military, if you got caught crying, you'd be harassed. Andrew learned that in his first week away from home. He was ready to serve his country and proud to do it. His parents were probably even more proud of him for doing his part to protect the country.

Missing his family got to him one night while in the barracks, and the tears just came. He thought he was being silent, but not silent enough for his bunkmate, who started taunting him. Andrew didn't say anything. He was tough and perfectly capable of defending himself, but he chose his battles wisely. This wasn't one he was interested in. He shut down and silenced his whimpering, at least until Ramirez, the loudmouth future politician in the bunk next to him, chimed in.

"Hey, if Simmons wants to cry a little 'cause he misses his family, you shut the fuck up and let him. It doesn't matter if the man has emotions. What matters is if he has your back as much as you have his when it counts. You say another thing to him, I'll come off this bunk and kick your teeth down your throat," Ramirez said, glaring at the soldier on the bottom bunk. Andrew didn't hear another word from that soldier for the rest of his deployment. That moment also marked the start of Andrew and Ramirez's friendship, and Andrew's introduction to the group that would become his best friends.

So, the shower is where Andrew let himself cry. Tonight, he cried in the shower like a newborn, letting the water wash all his tears down the drain. The sound of the water, along with the dryer still running, drowned out his cries. Andrew finishes up his shower and his cry session. He usually felt better afterward, like he was releasing all the bad inside him for a bit. But this time was different. It didn't relieve anything. Tonight was different from any other night before.

Andrew gets out of the shower and wipes the steam off the sink mirror. The tears are gone now, but he's left with bloodshot eyes. He stares in the mirror, using his fingertips to trace his scars down his neck, over his shoulder, down his arm, and along his ribs. To this day, he's still shocked he didn't die from the shrapnel that penetrated his body, especially along his ribs. The doctors kept reminding him how lucky he was to be alive. But every time he heard those words, he wished he wasn't that lucky. He wished he had the same luck as his small platoon that day.

Andrew's gaze is interrupted by the sound of the dryer's alert going off. He puts on the boxers and beater he grabbed earlier, then makes his way to the dryer and opens the door. He neatly folds the clothes and places them on top of the dryer. He grabs a pair of jeans and puts them on. He comes across his favorite thermal undershirt and slips it over his head. As he slides his arms through the sleeves, he feels the rough fabric graze the scars on his left arm. Andrew finishes folding the rest of the clothes and puts them away in his dresser. He goes back to the dryer and pulls out his military jacket. He runs his fingers over the Simmons patch and the other patches. Each one sparks a memory he doesn't like. He puts the jacket on and heads back to his bed. Sitting on the edge, he mixes another drink, noticing the rum bottle is now half empty. He takes a drink before leaning over and putting on his socks and boots. Then, he stands and heads back to the bathroom mirror. Looking at himself in the mirror.

At least your clothes are clean and mom won't be left with any dirty clothes to wash. You should probably shave and trim your hair. You do look homeless. Mom doesn't need to see you that way.

Andrew thinks to himself as he grabs the electric clippers sitting on the sink. His buzz is pretty strong, but he's already made up his mind to shave. He takes the clippers to his beard first. No real plan on shaping anything, just removing it. He runs the clippers all over his face as the strands of blonde and grey hair fall into the sink. He then adjusts the guard on the clippers before running it through the hair on his head. Again, with no plan. Just making it shorter and himself more presentable. He finishes cutting his hair and grabs the straight razor from the other side of the sink.

Andrew opens the straight razor and holds it up to his throat, just below his Adam's apple. He pauses for a second and takes a deep breath. *This is it. You know that, right?* he thinks to himself. He moves the razor up his Adam's apple, removing the remaining hair on his neck. He uses the razor to remove the stubble left behind on his jawline and up. He notices that the scars on his face are more visible with no hair. He second-guesses his decision to shave it all off. He's already committed to cutting it off and having a clean cut before the night is over. Andrew finishes shaving and closes the razor up before cleaning out the sink. He takes one last look at himself before heading out of the bathroom and back to his bed. He lays down on the bed on his back, crossing his legs and crossing his arms over his chest. He sits in silence as he stares again at the ceiling. He reaches for his phone, sees that the time is now 10:41. He holds down the side button and swipes the screen to shut off his phone for the night.

Andrew numbingly lies in his bed, his eyes focused on the ceiling. This action has become a comfortable part of his life in the last year. He sits in the silence, only the sounds of the old house's creaking wood expanding and contracting. There is a soft breeze outside, causing the leaves on the ground to lightly tap the window. He runs his hand over his freshly shaved face, feeling the scars again. He clenches his hand into a fist and punches himself in the chest, the pain of the scars hurting more than the thuds of his fist he is inflicting on himself. He turns over to his side and grabs the bottle of Admiral Nelson's, twisting the top off and tossing it on the nightstand. He grabs the Styrofoam cup and tilts the bottle to pour some of the rum inside it.

NINE

TONIGHT IS THE LAST NIGHT *I will ever do this. Tonight is the last night I will ever pour this shit in a cup,* Andrew thinks to himself, the reality of everything creeping in. He sets the cup back down and puts the bottle to his lips, taking a few large gulps straight from the bottle.

Why the fuck am I shaking and feeling this way? I've been planning this night for months. I've already talked myself into this. I think I'm just getting the jitters, and my nerves are taking over. I need to stop being a pussy. This is what my family needs. They don't need a zombie walking around ruining their lives, Andrew thinks to himself as he takes another swig from the bottle.

He looks at the bottle as he pulls it away from his lips. The bottle is now only a quarter full, and his buzz is quickly becoming a drunk. He sets the bottle down with a shaky hand. He sits up on the side of the bed, taking a moment to let his eyes catch up with the rest of his body. Once he is confident that the room is not spinning that badly, he attempts to stand up. As he stands, the drunkenness brings him back down to the edge of the bed. He almost misses the bed but catches himself with his hands. He lightly laughs to himself before attempting to stand again. This time, he makes it to his feet. He stands still for a moment while he gets his eyes in line with his body, swaying. After he gathers his sense of balance, he slowly makes his way over to the cardboard boxes stacked up next to the washer. He removes the top box and gently sets it to the side, making sure to be quiet. Andrew removes the blanket that is in the next box. Under the blanket was a weathered orange extension cord.

Andrew retrieves the extension cord and makes his way back to the bed, where he sets it down at the foot of the bed. He looks up above him at the wooden cross beam on the ceiling, right at the foot of the bed. Looking up causes him to lose his balance and stumble backward a few feet. He catches himself before falling to the ground. Gathering himself again, he makes his way back to the beam. He looks up at the beam with the two-inch hole drilled in it. His dad had drilled that hole twenty years ago to hang up a heavy bag when he was teaching Andrew how to fight. The bag came down many years ago. The hole will serve a different purpose tonight.

Andrew extends his arm to place his hand on the beam as an extra bit of stability. Luckily, his five-foot-nine-inch frame was just the right height to reach the bottom of the beam, eight feet off the floor. He stumbles back to the bed and picks the extension cord up. He unwinds it and grabs the male plug part of the cord. He stretches up and guides the plug through the hole.

Andrew threads the extension cord through the hole in the wooden beam overhead, pulling it taut until just enough length remains to form a noose. He carefully twists and knots the cord, adjusting it until the makeshift noose dangles securely in place, its length shortened to perfection. His Boy Scout troop leader would be so proud of the knot he formed while drunk. Andrew was just as proud of it. He stood there, staring at it and visually measuring the distance that it hung above the ground, trying to decide if it was far enough away from the ground to serve its purpose without his feet catching him on the floor and supporting his weight, making it useless.

Andrew stands right under the plastic and copper noose. He looks up at it. It's only about a head taller than he is, but that's perfect. He grabs the extension cord above the knot and gives it a few healthy yanks. In his mind, ensuring that the beam wouldn't break, which he knew it wouldn't. More importantly, he wanted to make sure there wasn't a whole lot of noise, just in case his body naturally wanted to survive and escape. The first few yanks proved that there was no noise. To make sure that his mother wouldn't wake up to any strange noises from the basement, he yanked on the extension cord more erratically. Still, there was no noise. Andrew was confident that his apparatus would be sufficient for tonight.

Andrew, satisfied, turns back towards the bed and climbs back in it. He grabs the bottle with a shaking hand, closing one eye to focus on the bottle. He places the bottle to his lips and lets out a long breath of air. He takes another long swig of the remaining rum in the bottle. He sets the bottle back down and lays on his back. He stares at the noose, slightly swaying on the beam. He can't tell if it's the noose itself swaying or if it's the whole room beginning to sway.

He closes his eyes in an attempt to stop the room from spinning around him. Eyes closed, his life begins to play out like a dream while awake. He remembers all the memories he shared with his family and friends. He remembers all the moments with his father. All the moments in time that eventually became life lessons. Even though in those moments, it was Charles correcting his behavior and attitude. All the moments that he spent with Izzy when she was younger. All the times his friends or girlfriends would want to hang out and go do something, but he couldn't because he was doing something with his little sister. They would be mad about it, but Andrew never was. He enjoyed watching her smile and giggle over anything they had planned. His mom ran through his head. How strong she was when his dad died. She didn't have to be. She was sensitive and relied on him for everything. When he died, it was like an internal switch just flipped. She became the provider, protector, and teacher.

He remembered the times that he spent with the small group of friends that he made on deployment. All the calls when they were apart. The FaceTimes and the planned get-togethers they had frequently. How much they would complain about the military but throw on those greens and make the best of every deployment they were sent on.

All those thoughts running through his mind were nice, and he enjoyed the images of everyone smiling. Just as fast as they swooped in, they disappeared and were replaced by all the sorrowfulness that now consumed Andrew's life. The moments his father taught him those life lessons turned into the moments he wasn't there for. All the moments that Andrew needed his guidance, and he was left tossing a ball in the air, talking to a ghost. All the moments that he wasn't there for Izzy while he was on deployment or the past year. The way that he knew it made her feel, because their father's absence made him feel the same way. How, ever since his dad passed, his mom wasn't the same woman she once was. She tried so hard to fill those shoes he left behind but lost herself in the process. He thought about all of his friends from the military. They were so close, and they all just vanished, all at the same time. No support from one another to mourn the loss of one of them. Andrew was left alone to mourn all of them all at once. The scars that were left behind on his body are a constant reminder of their last day together. The scars left behind on his mind and his soul are deeper than any mark on him.

These are the thoughts and the feelings that Andrew has become used to. They rip him apart mentally. He'd tried for a year to drown them in liquor. To cover them up with pills. To talk through them with his therapist. Nothing silenced them or numbed the feelings. As strong as his father, he was not. He was still that weak teenage boy his father left behind. This was the moment that he needed to be strong. He squeezed his eyes shut tighter, causing a tear to squeeze out of each one of his eyes. He opens his eyes and raises his hands to wipe the tears away. He takes a deep breath in and sits up. Andrew grabs the bottle of remaining rum and swallows it down. He looks at the empty bottle and sets it down. He stands up, stumbling. He catches himself and walks around to the foot of the bed, grabbing onto the noose to stabilize himself for a moment. He lets go of the noose and bends over slightly at the foot of the bed, lifting the mattress and bed spring up slightly to grab one of the milk crates that were supporting it. He lets the bed down quietly on the offset milk crates. He gently taps the milk crate he took off with his foot to position it directly under the cord rope. He extends his arms into the air to make contact with the beam to make his step onto the black milk crate more stable. He steps up with one foot and hoists himself up. Still slightly swaying, he keeps himself in place with the support of the beam. He places his other foot on the crate. He lets go of the beam with one of his hands and grabs the noose, pulling it over his head. He feels a weight lifted off his chest. The comfort and peace that he has been searching for seemed to be in the center of that loop. He uses the same hand to tighten up the knot on the back of his neck enough that when he drops, it'll catch and tighten up the rest of the way.

He lets go of the beam and balances himself on the milk crate. He uses his body weight to rock the crate back and forth a few times. He doesn't plan on an exact moment to kick it out from under himself. He figured he would let chance make that decision for him. The crate teeters at a high angle. Andrew closes his eyes, anticipating the jerk. His eyes are quickly snapped open as he hears the door to the basement open up and sees light from the kitchen start to beam through the darkness.

TEN

MICHAEL RUNS ON THE TREADMILL, his feet pounding away as the belt moves under his bare feet. One of the rooms in his suite has been transformed into a small gym. For some reason, one of the rules of the Pendulum Towers is to exercise daily. Michael follows all the rules the best he can. He has to follow them, or else.

The TV on the wall doesn't seem to play any new shows or movies. It only seems to be programmed to play those from his early life, which has its bonuses. He grew up in the 80s, one of the best decades. He runs on the treadmill watching *Die Hard*. He likes to picture himself as John McClane, and the only thing he wants to do is kill Hans Gruber, played by the diabolical asshole, Mr. B. Lial.

He once tried to escape by throwing a chair through the window. It proved useless; the windows were indestructible. So, he runs and imagines the day he gets the opportunity to leave this place—and maybe the chance to toss Mr. B. Lial off the edge.

He finishes his run on the machine and powers it down. He gulps down a bottle of water as the belt slowly comes to a stop before he steps off. He grabs a towel off the wall and walks closer to the TV as his favorite part is coming on. He watches it in silence, a smile on his face.

He hears the doorbell ring. Choosing to ignore it, he glances at the front door, then back at the TV. A second ring resonates through the suite. "I'll be there in a minute!" he yells, his eyes focused on the movie. The bell rings a third time. This time, the TV shuts itself off. Michael should have known—you answer the door when it rings. No exceptions. You get three rings, and then everything in the suite seems to shut itself off. Seraphin explained to him that it's just the rules. It's disrespectful to keep a guest waiting. Disrespect at the Pendulum Towers would not be tolerated, and accountability would be had.

"Okay, I get it. Sorry, I'm on my way now!" Michael yells as he makes his way out of the exercise room, into the hallway, and down to the front door. He twists the lock and opens it. Just like usual, no one is out there. The only person who comes to the suite is Seraphin, and she always announces herself at the door. Michael looks down and sees the silver platter with a silver dome cover over a plate. A silver knife and fork are wrapped up in a black napkin next to the plate on the right, and a silver cup with a silver lid is on the left. He sets the almost-empty bottle of water on the floor and picks up the platter. He steps back into his suite. Glancing down the hallway, he sees the same platters sitting in front of the other doors. He doesn't venture outside his suite anymore without Seraphin as an escort.

He attempted it a few months ago, just to knock on one of the doors down the hallway to see if he was not alone here. It feels like he is more and more alone with every day that passes. He had only taken a few steps outside his door when his feet began sinking into the floor. After a few more steps, waist-deep in what had turned into quicksand, he had to turn around and grab the edge of his door to pull himself back into his own personal hell.

He uses one hand to slowly close the door, peeking out through the crack as it shuts to see if he can catch a glimpse of one of the other doors opening. They never do, and they don't this time either. The door shuts completely, and he locks the deadbolt. He heads back down the hallway to the kitchen, where he sets the silver platter on the small island. The island only has two chairs. He's never really sure why there are two chairs. He figures the second one is reserved specifically for Seraphin. She's the only person who has ever sat across from him during his time here. Michael's already lost track of how long he's been here. He knows it's been months, but has it been a year yet? He really has no clue.

Michael takes his seat at the island and opens the cup, peering inside before taking a sniff. It's the same thing it always is after a workout: a chocolate and peanut butter protein shake, his favorite. He drinks it down, the chalky, thick texture familiar to him. He remembers a lot from his life—everything except the last few days. Those memories seem to have vanished from his mind. Still, he knows he misses his kids, and that's what keeps him going every day—the chance to get back to them, to wrap them in his arms, to apologize for being gone, and to hope for their forgiveness.

He finishes the protein shake and places the cup down with a small tink as the silver cup meets the platter. Lifting the silver dome from the plate, he reveals the same meal he always gets post-workout: a perfectly seared ribeye steak, broccoli, and sweet mashed potatoes—the ideal balanced meal. Michael grabs the fork and knife, cuts a piece of steak, and chews, savoring the flavor as usual. His gaze drifts to the black screen of the small TV mounted across from the island. It flickers to life and resumes playing *Die Hard* from where it left off in the exercise room—a sign that Michael is obeying the rules, being the good boy he's supposed to be.

Michael finishes his meal as the movie reaches its conclusion. Once done, he rises, heads to the front door, unlocks it, and opens it. He peers out, noting with a small smile that the other two silver platters in the hall are now gone. It's a subtle reminder that he's not completely alone here. He places his empty platter on the floor in front of his door, then makes his way to the master bedroom.

As he enters, he notices a small wrinkle in the bottom-left corner of the bedcover. Without hesitation, he tucks it in, smoothing it out. Making the bed perfectly, a habit drilled into him by the military, one he had neglected after getting out, but is now forced to relive here. It's one of the rules. "Your bed must be made every morning after you wake up. You're not an animal. If you want to be an animal, you'll be treated like one," he hears Seraphin's voice echo in his head. Satisfied with his work, he moves on to the master bathroom.

Michael steps into the open shower, washing off the sweat from his workout. When finished, he towels off. As he does, the bathroom lights flicker. Michael freezes, staring at his reflection in the mirror. He knows what's coming. The image of the bathroom slowly fades into blackness, replaced by smoke and glowing embers. Emerging from the haze is Mr. B. Lial.

"Hans," Michael mutters, before coughing to cover up the slip. "I mean, Mr. B. Lial. So nice to see you again," he adds sarcastically.

Mr. B. Lial stands in the mirror, rubbing his hands together. He's dressed in a sharp purple suit, with a light pink tie over a black shirt.

His fingers and wrists are adorned with diamond rings and bracelets. He chuckles softly, flashing a wide white smile that starkly contrasts his dark skin.

Michael chuckles back, drying his hair as he does. Mr. B. Lial's laughter grows louder, and Michael mirrors his energy, chuckling even louder in return. Suddenly, Mr. B. Lial waves a finger slowly, cutting off his laughter as though flipping a switch. In that instant, Michael lets out a scream of pain, dropping the towel and clutching his hand. His pinky finger is broken, twisted grotesquely off to the side.

"What the fuck?" Michael asks in agony.

"You know the rules, Michael. Respect is key here. It's disrespectful not to address someone as they wish to be addressed. You know my name. You will address me as it. There are consequences for our actions," Mr. B. Lial replies to him with his deep, hollow voice.

"It was a joke," Michael replies, still holding his shaking hand. "I know your damn name."

Mr. B. Lial's voice lowers in pitch with a grumbling echo. "Then address me as such! You may not like me, but you will respect me and my tower. Do you understand me?" Mr. B. Lial yells his question at Michael.

"Yes, I understand. I'm sorry, it won't happen again," Michael replies.

The smile returns to Mr. B. Lial's face as his posture becomes more relaxed. He waves his finger in front of him again as he says, "Thank you, Michael."

Michael grips his hand again in agony as another sharp pain shoots through his hand. He looks down at it. His pinky is now aligned as normal, the throbbing of the broken bone slowly being replaced by a very warm sensation. Michael grabs the white T-shirt off the sink and slides it over his head before sliding his arms through the sleeves carefully with his right hand.

"Now that all of that is behind us, how is everything going here at the Pendulum Towers? Are you getting everything you want, and is it to your satisfaction? How have your talks with Seraphin been?" Mr. B. Lial asks Michael, never losing the wide grin on his face.

Well, I would really like to be the fuck out of wherever the fuck this is, and I would really like to toss your sorry ass out of one of these windows, Michael thinks to himself, but doesn't dare say it out loud. "Things are going good, I guess. The food is good. Everything is a little repetitive. Seraphin has been very informative," he replies instead.

Mr. B. Lial tilts his head a little bit. "Michael, would you say that your stay so far has been satisfactory? I need to know."

Afraid of what the consequences would be of saying things have not been satisfactory, Michael simply replies with, "Yes, everything has been satisfactory," in a very dull tone.

Mr. B. Lial ecstatically claps his hands. "Excellent, Michael. That makes me very pleased to hear you say we are meeting your expectations here at the Pendulum Towers." He sighs for a quick second and looks up. "I strive for excellence, and it shows in your answer that we are excellent here." Mr. B. Lial claps his hands again.

What in the fuck is wrong with this guy? Excellence? I'm nothing more than a prisoner here, Michael thinks to himself as he stares blankly at Mr. B. Lial, still not sure if he can hear his thoughts or not. There have been times where it seemed like he did, but that could have been in his head.

"Yeah, everything is going great," Michael says with no emotion in his voice.

"Well, I think that's it for our time. I just wanted to stop by and make sure we are indeed living up to your expectations. Two contracts complete and two souls now mine. Good job, Michael. I enjoy the show," Mr. B. Lial says to Michael, laughing at him.

Of course, you enjoy the show, you sick fucker. You really enjoy watching people take their own lives, Michael thinks to himself. He replies with a simple, "Yep."

Mr. B. Lial pauses a moment, like he was expecting something more from Michael. Or, he heard his thoughts. "Looking forward to the next one, Michael," he says with a bit more evil in his voice.

The lights flicker in the bathroom again as Mr. B. Lial disappears into the darkness of the mirror before it transitions back to a normal mirror, and Michael sees himself standing there. He steps to the mirror and places his hands on the edge of the sink, hanging his head in silence.

Chapter

ELEVEN

I GOTTA GET OUT OF HERE. There has to be a way out. I don't know how many more times I can look into the eyes of someone that wants to end their life. I don't know how many more times I can kill myself before I completely lose my mind, he thinks to himself. He lifts his head and looks at himself in the eyes. *You'll do it as many times as it takes to get back to your kids. Now shut the fuck up and brush your teeth.*

Michael reaches for the toothbrush and toothpaste. He brushes his teeth and rinses his mouth with the spearmint-flavored mouthwash. He walks out of the bathroom, shutting the light off before closing the door.

He walks into the living room of the suite. Everything is so clean and so "new age." The furniture is nothing like what he had in his house. He sits in the chair in the corner of the room. A big, comfy, grey chair with a tall back. Positioned in the corner perfectly with a small nightstand to the left of it with a decanter of whiskey and one glass. To the right is a bookshelf that takes up the rest of the wall. Michael sits in the chair in his white T-shirt and boxer briefs. He didn't have a reason to put on any of the clothes that were provided in the closet or in the drawers of the dresser. No one was going to come and visit unless it was Seraphin, and she didn't really seem to care about much other than the tower.

Michael pours himself a half glass of whiskey from the decanter. He sips the liquid, feeling the sting of the alcohol as it travels down his throat and starts a warm fire in his belly. He looks over at the bookshelf and sees a book he hasn't seen before. He reaches for it and pulls it out. Holding it in his hands, he reads the words on the green cover: *How To Pray*. He glances down to check out the author and reads *Mr. B. Lial*. Michael looks around the room and thinks to himself, *I bet this is interesting. Where the hell did it come from?*

Michael hesitantly opens the book and skips through the first couple of blank pages. He gets to the first page of the actual book. Only one word is on the page in big, bold letters in the center of the page: *DON'T*. He turns the page. The next page is the same, bold style letters in the center of the page: *PRAY*. He flips to the next page: *IT* is all that is written. He grabs the pages in his hand and folds them, using his thumb to fan through the pages. One word per page, repeating the same sentences over and over again: *DON'T PRAY IT IS POINTLESS MICHAEL. YOUR SOUL IS MINE TO KEEP.*

Michael rips the pages out of the book and throws them in the air in front of him. The book lights up in a glowing orange hue, as well as the pages floating in the air. All the pages levitate in the air before the book acts like a vacuum and sucks them all back up into the book. The book then slams shut in Michael's hands. Startled by what happened, Michael jumps in his seat and shoves the book back in its home on the bookshelf. He then grabs the drink next to him and chugs it.

He sits in the chair for a moment, with his heart racing as he stares out the window across the room. Nothing is out there. The only thing outside is a deserted basin with sharp, rocky mountains and small fires as far as Michael can see. The doorbell goes off and startles Michael in his stare. This time, the bell chime is immediately followed by Seraphin's soft voice.

"Michael, it is Seraphin. Please open the door."

Michael promptly stands up and heads to the front door. He has learned that Seraphin does not like to wait until the third notification before she is acknowledged.

Michael gets to the door, quickly unlocks the deadbolt, and turns the handle to open it. Standing there is Seraphin in her grey and black concierge uniform. Her perfectly braided hair nested perfectly in a large bun on her head. Her perfect almond skin highlighted by accents of makeup. Her scar on her neck is still not completely covered by the foundation that she uses. She smiles her big, bright, warm, and inviting red lipstick smile.

Seraphin's smile always makes Michael feel a little bit better about his situation.

"Hello, Michael. I understand everything has been satisfactory so far during your stay with us," she says with a smile and bubbly voice.

"Yes, of course it has," Michael replies. He looks down past Seraphin's intense green eyes and notices that she has a suit neatly folded in her arms, with a small envelope sitting on top of it. He looks back up at her.

"Is it time? It's been a while since the last one," he asks her.

"Well, of course it's time, Michael. No time to waste. Please change and meet me in the study," Seraphin says. She had a bad habit of saying "of course" a lot. It was an idiosyncrasy of hers that Michael didn't really mind, but noticed every time she did it.

Seraphin takes the small letter from the top of the clothes and places it in her blazer pocket. She hands the outfit to Michael and walks past him, opening a door to the right in the hallway and shutting the door behind her.

Michael pauses for a second, still getting used to the formality of everything at the Pendulum Towers. There was never time for chit-chat. He catches himself just standing there. He shuts the door and walks down the hallway, through the master bedroom, to the master bathroom. He slides on the black slacks, slides his arms through the sleeves of the silk white button-down shirt, tucks it in, and buckles the belt. He buttons the cuffs on the shirt sleeve before grabbing the jacket and sliding it over the silk shirt. He buttons the two buttons before sliding on the shoes. He glances at himself in the mirror. The same outfit he wore the last two times. He takes a deep breath before exiting the bathroom and making his way to the study.

He opens the door and walks in. The room is empty except for a silver table in the middle. He's still not sure why it's referred to as a study. It's more of a briefing and torture room. Seraphin is standing opposite of him at the silver table. Her posture is perfect, looking down at the table. Michael steps in front of the table, opposite of her. Seraphin looks up.

"Are you ready, Michael?" she asks him.

"I guess so, do I have an option?" he replies back to her.

"Of course," Seraphin replies, not answering Michael's question. She pulls the small envelope out of her blazer pocket, sits it on the large silver table, and slides it over closer to Michael.

Michael grabs the envelope and lifts it up. He rips the edge off and pulls out the small card inside. He sets the ripped envelope down on the table and looks at Seraphin, who stands in front of him like a statue. He takes the card inside and holds it in one hand as he lifts the top part of the card up. The same thing as the last time. Only two words on the card in graceful calligraphy writing.

ANDREW SIMMONS

Chapter

TWELVE

MICHAEL FOLDS THE CARD BACK up and places it back in its envelope. He sits on the silver table. Michael and Seraphin make eye contact and nod at each other, signaling that Michael has the name memorized. The card and envelope on the table ignite into flames and burn quickly, before turning into a small pile of ashes.

Seraphin removes a small brush and silver dustpan out of her blazer pocket. She sweeps the ashes into the dustpan and closes the lid to contain the ashes inside. She then places them both back into her pocket.

"Very well, Michael. You have the information. Is there anything you need from me?" she asks Michael after placing her smile back on her face.

"I hate this. I hate it every time. Do you have any idea what it's like to do what I'm being forced to do?" Michael asks as he slightly lowers his head.

"Of course, Michael. I do know what it's like. Remember, however, you're not being forced. You signed the contract. You made the choi—"

Michael interrupts her, slamming the palms of his hands down on the table. "I didn't have a choice!" he exclaims. "It was either this or what? Forever in this hell?"

Seraphin, unfazed by the sudden outburst from Michael, finishes what she was saying before being rudely interrupted. "Choice. You made the choice. We all have the ability to make our own decisions and choices. Of course, some of those choices do not play out as we intend them to. I do know what it's like. I made my choice as well, Michael. Trust me, the Pendulum Towers is the hell a soul would wish for."

Seraphin takes a moment of silence to ensure that Michael is focusing on what she is saying.

"Do not interrupt me while I'm speaking again. It is very disrespectful. Now, please see your guest to the door," she finishes as she extends her arm out with her palm up, as if pointing to the door, anticipating Michael to turn around and open it.

Michael stares at Seraphin, wanting to say so much. He still has so many questions. Every time he asks one, he just gets a simple, grey answer. After a moment, Michael turns around and opens the door to the study.

He gestures to Seraphin to follow him. "Of course," he says as he stands with the door open.

Seraphin wraps around the table and exits past Michael. She heads down the hallway to the front door as Michael follows her. Seraphin stops at the front door as she waits for Michael to unlock the deadbolt and open the door for her. He opens the door and steps back.

Seraphin exits out the door and turns around to face Michael. "Get a little bit of rest and prepare your mind, Michael. It will soon be time," she says to Michael as she lowers her head, indicating the conversation is over and that it's okay to shut the door.

Michael shuts the door and deadbolts it. He turns back around and heads down the hallway into the living room, where he takes a seat back on the comfy tall-backed chair in the corner.

Michael pours himself another drink from the decanter and swallows it all down in one stinging gulp. He sits in silence, staring out the window into the rocky hills of flames. This was his preparation—sitting in silence and drinking, getting lost in his thoughts. He had no idea who Andrew Simmons was or what he was dealing with in life. He had no idea who Charlie or Donna were either when he read their names on those cards. He learned quickly who they were, though.

Michael sits there with a drink in his hand, slowly sipping it, trying to picture in his mind who this Andrew was. He could run a thousand different scenarios in his mind, and every one of them would be wrong. He knew what his contract fulfillment meant if he was successful, and he wasn't looking forward to that either. So Michael sits, running scenario after scenario through his mind, getting lost in his thoughts. Lost in the time that has passed.

Michael is brought out of his trance by the doorbell chiming through the suite. All the lights begin flickering and transitioning from their soft white to a soft red. Michael knows the time has come. He stands up and drinks the last bit of liquor in his glass. He tugs on his blazer bottom and ensures the buttons are still buttoned. He adjusts the cuffs of his sleeves and gives the collar of his shirt a small tug up. He exhales as he walks down the hallway to the front door. He slowly unlocks the deadbolt and twists the handle, mentally preparing himself for what's about to happen.

Michael slowly opens the door. He peers out the door as it opens. The scenery is no longer the hallway with the two doors down the way. Michael looks down at a flight of wooden stairs leading to a concrete floor at the bottom. The smell of cheap whiskey and mildew suddenly hits him in the face. He slowly takes a step onto the first stair and closes the door behind him. He walks down the wooden stairs slowly and softly, the wood barely creaking under his feet. He gets near the bottom of the stairs and is able to see the corner of a bed with what appears to be milk crates as the bed frame. Another step down the stairs reveals a man standing on one of those milk crates with an extension cord wrapped around his neck.

Michael was right. None of the thousand scenarios were the right one.

THIRTEEN

ANDREW STABILIZES THE MILK CRATE under his feet and grabs the extension cord around his neck. His heart pounds in his chest at the thought that it's his mom or little sister coming down the stairs. He struggles with removing the noose as he peers at the staircase and tilts his head as he sees what appears to be a shiny pair of black shoes followed by a pair of ironed black suit pants slowly coming down the stairs. Andrew starts to think he's hallucinating, blinking his eyes repeatedly to try to shake the hallucination. The blinks don't help shake the image of the man walking down the stairs slowly.

Andrew finally wrestles his way loose from the noose. He grabs onto it with both hands. "Who, who the hell are you?" he asks the stranger on the staircase, his voice quiet and erratic. Even in Andrew's confusion, he keeps his voice down so as not to wake his family.

Michael, now at the bottom of the stairs, eye level with Andrew, throws his hands up in a friendly, not-armed gesture and stops in his tracks.

Michael responds in a soft, calm voice. "Hey, I'm just a friend. I'm not here to cause you any harm, I promise."

Andrew steps down from the milk crate, still holding onto the extension cord to stabilize himself. Once his feet are on the ground and he feels like he's not going to topple over, he lets go of the noose. "I don't know you, man. I've never seen you in my life. How the hell did you get in here? I didn't hear any footsteps upstairs," Andrew says, positioning himself in a hand-to-hand combat stance.

Michael, with his hands still in the air, says, "Like I said, I'm just a friend, Andrew. That's all. Just a friend."

Andrew squints his eyes at the mysterious man on the stairs. "How do you know my name? Is my family okay?"

"I can't really tell you how I know your name. Yes, if your family is here, I promise they are safe. It will be very difficult for me to explain how I got here. I'm not really sure either. My name is Michael Atone. I'm just a friend. Is it okay if I put my hands down and have a seat on the stairs?" Michael asks.

Andrew doesn't respond. He just nods his head, feeling himself sway a little bit. *What in the fuck? Am I hallucinating, or just really drunk?* Andrew asks himself.

Michael slowly unbuttons his blazer and sits down on the bottom step. He doesn't drop his hands to his knees until he is seated.

"Please sit, Andrew," Michael says, noticing him slowly swaying side to side.

"Nah, I have no idea who the fuck you are. I'll stand, and you tell me exactly who you are. Or things are going to get real loud in here," Andrew says as he shakes his head, his vision blurring.

"I'm just a friend. That's all I can tell you right now, Andrew. I'm just a friend who is here to help in a moment when you need one. My name is Michael. I'm just here to talk," Michael explains, attempting to ease Andrew's mind.

Andrew glares at Michael, focusing on his face. He does look kinda familiar. He just doesn't have the beard and long hair. "Wait, are you from the meeting? The dude with the gun. Did you follow me to my house? That's fucking creepy, man," Andrew says, confident this is the same Michael from the meeting earlier.

Michael slowly shakes his head. "I'm not sure what meeting you're talking about. I've never seen you before this moment," Michael answers.

"No, dude, it is you. You just don't have the shitty beard and long hair. Why the hell would you follow someone to their house? Not everyone needs saving. Just because you didn't pull the trigger doesn't give you the right to stalk people and sneak into their homes," Andrew says, his voice raising with agitation.

Michael raises his hands a little. "I promise we have never met. I don't know the meeting you're talking about. I don't know what trigger you're talking about. You're absolutely right— not everyone needs saving, but everyone deserves the opportunity to try to save themselves. That's all I'm here for." Michael points at the noose hanging from the beam. "It looks like that opportunity is right now. I'm just a friend, here to talk."

"Stop calling yourself my friend. I have no clue who you are. You're not my friend. All my friends are dead. Like I should be," Andrew replies, pointing his finger at Michael.

"Fine. If that's what you want, I'll stop saying I'm your friend," Michael replies, tilting his head in a questioning gesture. "What do you mean your friends are all dead?" he asks.

Andrew pauses and rubs his head with his hands. "I mean they're dead, man. How many things can someone mean by that? They're dead. They died. They're no longer alive. Is that clear?" Andrew throws his hands in the air and sarcastically tilts his head.

"They're dead, and I'm still here when I shouldn't be."

Michael pauses for a second. "Okay. Tell me about them. Why are you supposed to be dead also?" Michael asks.

Andrew exhales harshly. His emotions transitioned from fear and shock to anger and discomfort. "They're dead, man. They all blew up in an attack while we were in some other country protecting and helping their people. Our people died. My people died. I was a coward and jumped out of the Humvee. Does that make it clear?" Andrew runs his hands through his hair again, scratching his scalp.

"No, you told me how they died and how you lived. That's not what I asked. I want you to tell me about them and why you're supposed to be dead," Michael replies.

Andrew stares at Michael, annoyance covering his face. "Why the hell do you need to know about them? I was supposed to die with them. One for all and all for one. Instead, their families got a nice folded flag back, and my family got this scarred, sorry sack of shit coward back."

"I don't need to know about them. I want to know about them. How are you a coward for jumping out of the vehicle? It's horrible that their families sent off a child, parent, loved one, and got a flag back in their place. Your family got the man back. He may not be the same man and may think of himself as a coward. To your family and the people that love you, they got back way more than a flag," Michael says.

A silence fills the basement of Andrew's house for a few moments while the two men stare at each other. The ten feet between them felt like ten inches of space slowly closing in.

Andrew breaks the silence. "I should have died with them. They were my closest friends. I shouldn't have jumped out. I should have stayed and burned up with them. I should have come back as nothing more than a flag as well. Instead, my mom and sister got this monster in place of the perfectly folded flag. I should have died a hero as well." Andrew says as he lifts up his shirt to show the tiger stripes of scars along his rib cage.

Michael studies the scars for a brief moment before replying, "I see your scars. I don't think those are the scars that brought you to this moment. I think the scars on your heart and mind are way worse than those scars. Nobody will ever see them, but you have dealt with them since you got home. I did my tours as well and watched someone I had a lot of respect for die in front of me. It left a scar that will probably never heal. I remember him every day. Your family's soldier didn't die a hero. He's a living hero. Some people will never understand how, to some of us, that is worse than dying a hero."

Andrew pauses for a second and feels the tension in his shoulders start to lift away. The discomfort that he typically deals with in these situations is more bearable. "You had someone die while you were over there too?" Andrew asks Michael with a stutter, and a subtle sense of wanting to hear yes.

"I did," Michael responds with a small smile on his face as he remembers his sergeant. "It was my sergeant. A great guy. An asshole, actually, but a great guy all the same. He would do anything for his squad. He was demanding but understanding. He understood that not everyone was built the same way physically or mentally. The only thing he expected was for you to do your best and have your squad's six no matter what. If he felt you weren't giving something your all, he would call you on your bullshit. Ninety-nine percent of the time, he was right—you weren't giving your all. But he was sure to bring the best soldier and person in you out into the open."

Chapter

FOURTEEN

MICHAEL PAUSES FOR A MOMENT and wipes his face with his hand as he exhales. "We were on a routine recon mission. No threat at all. Drones had already flown through and didn't identify any enemies in our path for miles. We were a little more relaxed than we should have been. We were just walking along the alleyways, talking shop about anything other than our objective." Michael pauses again and hangs his head down a moment while he rubs his hands together. He lifts his head back up. "We took a right, less than three clicks from our target. Sarge was up front leading the way. I was behind him to the right. Collins was to the left. Three others were behind us. A small group for a small mission. We were laughing about something that I can't remember. All of a sudden, my eyes shut as I felt a warm liquid cover my face like I'd just been hit in the face with a warm water balloon that exploded on contact. Then there was a loud bang. We all got into formation with our rifles out." Michael pinches the top of his nose in between his eyes. He extends his arms as if he's pretending to hold an AR in front of him. "All of us, except for Sarge. He folded to the ground with a small hole in the left side of his forehead. We all dropped to one knee while Collins checked on him. Collins pulled his helmet off, and his brains just spilled out on the dirty gravel. I wiped my face and looked at my hand. That warm water balloon that exploded on my face was Sarge's blood. The bullet hit before we heard the bang."

Michael stares at his hand in front of his face, drops the invisible AR he was holding, and stares at his palms. Clean now, after many years, but still stained with that warm blood.

Andrew hangs his head without making eye contact. "I'm sorry, man. That's horrible." He lifts his head back up to see Michael still looking at his hand. "How did you get over it?" he asks.

"I didn't. I never got over it. Still not over it. I think about it all the time. It was hard, and still is hard, every once in a while. Some days are worse than others. But I like to check in on his family every once in a while and see how they are doing. On the anniversary of his death, I celebrate his life. I keep the person he was alive. That's how I deal with it," Michael answers, interlocking his hands together and nodding his head.

"I guess I never thought about it that way. I wish I could deal with it like you do. I wish I was strong enough. I'm not. I'm too weak. The thoughts of them dying flood my brain every time I think about them.

Then it just brings me down and makes me a stranger in my own head," Andrew replies.

"I understand the feeling of being a stranger in your own mind. Can you do me a favor, though? I want to try something with you," Michael asks.

"What's that?" Andrew asks in response. Michael extends his hand, palm up, towards the bed. "Please have a seat. I want you to close your eyes and try something that helped me."

Andrew hesitates before sidestepping to the corner of the bed, which still had the two milk crates holding it up. He sits down on the corner.

"I'll close my eyes. You stay right there." His face indicates there would be bad consequences if Michael approached while his eyes were closed.

"No worries. You have my word. I'll stay right here until you tell me it's okay to move," Michael reassures him, raising his hands in the air momentarily. Andrew slowly closes his eyes.

"Okay, now what?" Andrew asks.

"Think about your friends. Think about that day. Tell me what you see," Michael replies. "Man, I don't want to do this. I told you what I see," Andrew responds.

"I know you did. I know you have no reason, but trust me," Michael answers.

Andrew sniffs and swallows hard with his eyes closed. He begins telling Michael about that day. He describes sitting in the Humvee and where they were all sitting. Andrew tells him what they were talking and laughing about. All of them were laughing at Danny. Then came the sound of the windshield shattering and the sudden, brief scream from Danny as the missile lodged inside his chest, followed by the immediate silence of Danny's voice. Andrew starts to have tears run down his cheeks as his body begins to shake.

Michael notices the change in Andrew's composure.

"Stop right there. Go back a bit, to when you were telling me about all their plans," Michael interrupts Andrew's story.

Andrew wipes the tears from his cheeks without opening his eyes. He tells Michael the story again about everyone's plans and continues to the part where the windshield shatters.

Michael interrupts him again.

"Stop there. Tell me about their plans again."

Andrew pauses in his story. He opens his eyes to look at Michael, who is still sitting on the stairs with his arms crossed, leaning on his knees.

"Why do you want me to keep telling you about their plans? Their plans were ruined. Do you want to hear the story or not?" Andrew asks, his voice rising.

"Trust me, Andrew. Tell me the part about their plans again," Michael responds.

Andrew wipes his eyes and nose and closes his eyes again. He goes back into the story, telling the part about them laughing about their plans and Danny being an idiot. Every time Andrew gets to this point in the story, a small smile forms on his face before he gets wrapped up in the missile. Michael notices it every time, like a boxer noticing an opponent dropping his shoulder slightly before throwing a heavy hook.

Andrew tells the story for the third time and gets to the window shattering. Michael interrupts again.

"Stop there. Did you guys hang out together as a group at a bar or anything while on leave?" Andrew takes a deep breath.

"Of course we did," he replies, a bit of annoyance surfacing in his voice again. "Tell me about a time at a bar," Michael suggests.

Andrew goes into one of the many stories he has about him and the squad sitting around a table at one of the dozens of bars they visited while on leave. The table was covered in empty glasses and pitchers. Peanut shells everywhere. All of them were laughing and smiling. Michael sees the smile on Andrew's face start to form again while telling the story. A smile forms on Michael's face as well. Michael stops Andrew again. "Tell me about that night at the bar again. It sounds like you made a great group of friends and you all just clicked. I want to hear more about that story."

Andrew wipes the tears from his eyes and looks up at the ceiling of his basement. He has a smile on his face as he remembers in detail that one night at the bar. He even chuckles a few times while telling the story. Andrew exhales deeply as he finishes the story. He looks towards Michael with the same smile on his face.

"See that? Feel that? That's how you should remember them. You shouldn't let their ghosts haunt your memories. You should let those moments that you shared, laughing and strengthening that bond, flood over you when you think about them," Michael says to Andrew with a smile on his face as well. "I'm not going to say those thoughts of that day in the Humvee are not going to find a way to creep in and try to tear you down, 'cause I know all too well that they will. But the moment that you remember them in that way, you need to stop and force those memories from the days and nights together to blanket them. You don't have to forget that they died or how they died. Those thoughts are a very important part of who you are," Michael continues, moving his hands around as he speaks. "Those thoughts alone, though, are not who you are."

Andrew sits in silence for a moment, his lip quivering, holding back his tears. He rubs his hands together nervously.

"Do you really think I can do that? The thoughts are really strong sometimes," he asks Michael with a nervousness in his voice, searching for reassurance.

Michael smiles empathetically. "Of course I do, Andrew. You just showed me that you can. You had to do it with a little bit of guidance, but it won't always be that way," Michael reassures him. "A moment like that is hard to forget and shouldn't be forgotten. It also shouldn't be the only thing that consumes your thoughts. There's plenty of room in that mind for beautiful thoughts. You said that you had a sister. Would you want her memory to be consumed by something like what might happen tonight?" he asks Andrew.

Andrew exhales again. "I thought about that a lot before tonight as well." He pauses while he searches for the proper words to say. "No, I wouldn't want her to think about her brother hanging from a beam. Not one part of me wants her to think of that when I pop in her mind." He rubs his hands together again. "I... I also don't want her to think of me as the reclusive, scarred drunk that lives in the basement. The longer I wait to eliminate that person, the more memories she'll have of him," Andrew says as he sluggishly nods his head and begins to tear up again.

"I'm glad you brought that up. Is it okay if I come closer? I won't sit on your lap, but maybe that milk crate there," Michael asks jokingly as he points to the milk crate still sitting under the yellow noose.

Andrew debates with himself about letting the still stranger any closer to him. He just nods his head, agreeing to Michael's request.

"Perfect," Michael says as he stands up and slowly walks to the milk crate and takes a seat. "You said that you don't want her to remember you as this hermit that you have become. Who do you want her to remember you as? Tell me what the very next memory you want her to have of you is," Michael says to Andrew.

Andrew bites the inside of his lip as he thinks about the thoughts his little sister already has of him as this person. A small smirk creeps onto his face, remembering her just recently scrolling through a bunch of memories of him on her phone. He makes eye contact with Michael.

"I want her to remember the person that I was. I want her to remember all the times we hung out. I want her to remember all the times I was there for her, right by her side in every accomplishment she made. I want her to remember being right there by my side in every accomplishment that I made. I want her to remember me being strong and the person she looked up to," he says, tears rolling down his cheeks.

Michael leans in a little bit towards Andrew. "Is that what she will remember tomorrow after she walks down the stairs and sees the person she admired?" Michael asks.

Andrew reflects for a moment, then simply replies, "No."

"'No" is correct. What do you want her to remember tomorrow? Tomorrow isn't here yet. If you had to plan her memory for tomorrow tonight, what would it be?" Michael asks.

Andrew deliberates with himself for a moment. "I don't know what you mean. Like what do I want her to remember tomorrow morning? How the hell am I supposed to answer that?" Andrew asks irritably. "I want her to remember me… I don't know… doing anything," he continues.

Michael scoots towards Andrew. The milk crate makes a quiet grinding sound as it scoots across the concrete floor.

"Do you want her to remember you dangling from a cord? Your face white and your body limp. The coroner comes by and tells her what she already knows. The zipped-up black bag being hauled up the stairs by four strangers? Is that how you want her to remember you?" He asks Andrew, locking eyes with him and following his gaze as Andrew attempts to avoid eye contact.

"No, not at all," Andrew says aggressively as he clenches Michael's lapel in his fist. "I would never want that for her, never." He starts to whimper as he hangs his head.

Michael grabs Andrew's clenched fist around his lapel in his hand and slowly removes it. He holds his fist in his own hands. He can feel Andrew's hand trembling. "There's still time to change that memory, Andrew. There's still time to make new memories. You will never be the person that you once were again. You've been through a horrific event. You still have healing to do. But you can still be the person that she needs. You can still leave her with memories that she will be proud to have stored in her mind," Michael says to Andrew, gripping his hand, letting him know he's there for him.

Andrew slowly pulls his hand out of Michael's hands and uses it to wipe the tears off his eyes. He takes a deep breath. "Thank you. You're right. You're absolutely right. There is still plenty of time to make new memories. I'm not the person I once was, and I never will be again," Andrew says, with sadness flowing through every word. "But, I can be a better person than the person that I am now." He looks up at the extension cord dangling from the beam. "I can't believe this was almost the last memory I was going to leave them with." Andrew throws his hand up to cover his mouth as it all hits him that he was almost there. Just moments from being nothing more than a statistic and a bad memory for the people that he loved.

"Thank you again. I never intended for my life to end up here. It was just too much. Just too much. I'm still not sure how or why you ended up here, but I'm glad you did. You're an angel, man, I'll never forget you."

FIFTEEN

MICHAEL PAUSES FOR A MOMENT with a distant look on his face. "Good. I think you made the right choice tonight, Andrew. Your family needs you in their lives. More importantly, you have so much more to do in this life. Unfortunately, you won't remember me. This part of your memory will be replaced. I was never here. You made this decision on your own, Andrew. There's one more thing for us to do before I leave," Michael says to him.

Andrew glares at him with a puzzled look on his face. "What do you mean I won't remember you and you were never here? What else do I need to do?"

Michael replies, "You just won't, that's how it works. I'm not here to be remembered. It's not my fate. I do need you to stand up, though."

Andrew, still puzzled, stands up as Michael stands up. "Now what?" he asks Michael.

Michael buttons his blazer and fixes his collar. He turns around and looks at the noose right behind him. "You need to take this thing down."

Andrew, confused by the last bit of their conversation, steps towards the noose as Michael steps out of the way. He reaches up and begins to unknot it as he continues his conversation. "I'm not sure what the hell you mean by I won't remember you. How could someone possibly not remember something like this? Of course, I'm going to remember you, man. You saved my life. You know—" He interrupts himself as he finishes unknotting the noose and starts pulling it through the hole. He looks at Michael, who is no longer standing there.

Andrew glances at the stairs in time to see Michael's feet step up out of his view. The door slowly opens and then closes. Andrew doesn't hear any footsteps or any other doors open and close.

Andrew begins to take a step towards the stairs. Something inside him pulls him back and gives him the feeling that he doesn't need to investigate the silence upstairs. He turns around and takes off his coat and lays it across the bottom of the bed. He lifts the corner of the bed missing the milk crate foundation and uses his foot to slide it back into place. Andrew crawls into the bed and lays on his back and tucks his hands behind his head. He stares at the ceiling, motionless for a few moments. A smile slowly forms on his face as he closes his eyes and drifts off to sleep.

Andrew wakes up later in the morning and rubs the sleep out of his eyes. He sits up on the side of the bed and runs his hands through his hair. He looks over at the empty bottle of Admiral Nelsons sitting on the end table. *What the hell happened last night? I can't believe I was about to end everything. I'm glad I talked myself out of it.* Andrew thinks to himself. He gets up and heads up the stairs and opens the door to the kitchen. Inside the kitchen, Izzy and his mom are at the sink finishing up the dishes from their late breakfast. Izzy didn't have school on Thursdays so she spent it doing chores so she could have the weekend to just hang out and lounge.

They both turn around to Andrew opening the door.

"Andy, I'm surprised you're up this early. If I would have known. I would have made a little extra for breakfast," Andrew's mom says to him with a bit of shock on her face.

"It's no problem, mom. I'll just grab some cereal or something." He replies, as he walks around the island table to the sink. All three of them stare at one another in silence before Andrew extends his arms open wide and grabs both of them and draws them into a group hug. Izzy and Amanda grip onto Andrew tightly, enjoying this moment that doesn't happen very often. Iif even at all.

Andrew starts to cry a little bit, with his head tucked in between them. "I'm sorry guys, I'm sorry that I haven't been myself for the last year. I'm sorry that I'vebeen a burden on you guys. I need help. I've been having bad thoughts that have been hard for me to deal with. I thought they were too powerful and I was too weak to deal with them." Andrew cries even more into both of their shoulders.

"What are you saying, Andy?" Izzy asks as she rubs his back.

"I need you guys to believe me when I tell you I'm going to be okay. Last night, I set everything up to end my life. I felt like I wasn't the person I once was and I was doing nothing but dragging you guys down. Then, as I stood there about to let go. I had all these thoughts of the beautiful moments of my life pop in my head. Then I must have started talking to myself and I found the strong man inside of me that I thought was gone forever. I blinked and everything was clear. I don't want you guys to remember this person. I'm going to spend a very long time being the person you want to remember. I'm going to keep going to counseling and doing all the things to face my demons."

All three of them stay in the tight group hug sobbing and rubbing each other's backs. Amanda speaks up, with tears in her eyes. "Oh, Andy. You will always be our Andy. No matter what demons you're facing. We will always be there. You just need to talk to us and let us in. We love you so much."

Izzy wipes tears from her eyes and voices her feelings. "I will always remember you as the person who walked in dad's shoes when you didn't need to. You did that for me. I will always remember you as my best friend. Don't you ever, ever leave me. I need you more than you know." She says as she bawls.

Andrew lifts his head up and wipes the tears out of his eyes. "I know. I love you guys and need you more than you will ever know, as well." He says to them with a smile on his face, tears still in his eyes. "I'm gonna head back down stairs and shower up and start the day. Since you're off school, you wanna maybe go toss the ball around outside, Izzy? Then maybe tonight we can have another dinner… .as a family." Andrew asks Izzy as his eyes bounce between both of them. Izzy replies to Andrew. "I think I would like that. Be careful though, my fastball ain't nothin to mess around with." She says as she laughs, making the serious situation a bit softer.

Amanda, with a little chuckle in her voice at Izzy's comment, replies. "I would love to have a family dinner. Does the same time work?" She asks.

Andrew smiles again. He's smiled more this morning than he has in a very long time. "Sounds perfect mom,." he says as he turns around and heads towards the basement door.

Andrew opens the door and heads down the stairs. He stops at the small dresser and selects some clothes to change into after his shower. Andrew heads to the makeshift shower and turns it on, adjusting the temperature knobs until the water is just right. He then turns around and goes to the mirror. He wipes off the steam that has already started forming. Andrew takes off his shirt and tosses it in the hamper.

He sees the scars all over his left side in the mirror. He uses his right hand to trace some of the ones running up his arm onto his neck. Just yesterday, this would have been a moment that would have encouraged him to grab a bottle of rum and start the day off with a warm buzz. This time was different for Andrew. He looks at himself in the mirror and says out loud. "I miss you guys and I'll never forget what happened. I'll never forget the reason I have these scars. I won't allow them to dictate my life any longer. I'll use them to remember you in the moments I want to remember and I want to cherish." Andrew nods his head at himself in acknowledgement. He turns around and gets in the shower, closing the curtain behind him.

SIXTEEN

MICHAEL OPENS THE DOOR TO his suite and steps in. He looks out the doorway as he shuts it and sees the basement stairs of Andrew's basement start to fade out. He closes the door and locks the deadbolt. He walks a short way down the hallway and opens the study door to the right. The room is still empty but with a few extra items on the table. Michael closes the door behind him. He unbuttons his blazer and sets it on top of the silver table. On the table he sees an envelope, an extension cord, a pen, and a stool. Michael grabs the envelope and opens it, pulling out the card inside. *Andrew Simmons* is all it says on the top part of the card. Michael closes his eyes, emptiness consuming his thoughts and feelings. He opens them back up and sets the card back down on the table and grabs the pen. He twists off the top to reveal the fountain pen tip. He writes something on the bottom part of the card. He then adjusts his grip on the pen to hold it like a knife. He slowly sticks the fountain pen tip into his right thumb, until it breaks the skin and he begins to bleed. He looks at the blood for a moment to make sure there is enough. He then places his bloody thumbprint on the card below the words he had written.

Michael grabs the stool and places it on the ground. He then grabs the extension cord and looks up to see a beam that has never been in the room before. He steadies himself as he climbs on top of the stool. Michael works in silence as he tosses the extension cord over the beam and ties it into a noose. He widens the center of the noose as he slips it over his head. He reaches behind him to tighten it up, snug against his flesh. Michael takes a few deep breaths as tears form in his eyes. He uses his body weight to rock the stool back and forth. The stool eventually wobbles to a point where it slips out from under Michael's feet. Michael's body suddenly drops to the floor, his feet only about five inches over the ground. Michael's body convulses as he struggles to get air in his lungs. He grabs at the bottom of the noose tightly secured around his throat. He begins to kick his legs as his face gets tingly and everything begins to blur. Spit and snot escaping from his mouth and nose as he drags in the last bit of air into his lungs. He feels his lips tingle as he loses strength in his arms and they fall to his side. Michael lets out the last breath of air in his lungs as he drifts away. His body slowly swayed, lifeless.

A brief time passes and there is a buzz at the front door to Michael's suite. Seraphin opens the door and walks in. She heads directly to the study and opens the door. Inside she sees Michael's lifeless body dangling from the extension cord. She looks up at his face for a moment, then walks past him to the other side of the table. She grabs the card off the table and reads it to herself. The top part simply says *Andrew Simmons*. On the bottom part of the card is Michael's dried bloody thumbprint. Above that are four simple words. *Save One Lose One.*

Seraphin folds the card up and places it into the envelope. She sits it on the silver table and retrieves a match from her blazer pocket. She strikes the match and ignites the envelope. The paper burns up quickly and turns to ashes. Seraphin then takes a small dustpan and brush from her blazer pocket. She sweeps the ashes up into the dustpan. She retrieves a small silver container from her pocket. She dumps the ashes into the silver container and closes the lid of it. As soon as she closes the lid. The noose around Michael's throat suddenly vanishes and Michael's lifeless body drops to the ground with a thud.

Seraphin stands at attention with a blank stare on her face. A short interval of time elapses. Then the sound of Michael coughing echoes through the small room. Michael continues to cough as he places a hand on the silver table to pull himself up. He gasps for air as he makes his way to his feet. He stands on the other side of the table with both his hands on the table to help support his weight as his legs start to work again. Seraphin smiles wide as she typically does while addressing Michael. "Are you with me, Michael?" She asks.

Michael takes a few hard breaths and tries to answer her. His throat is so sore that he can't get the words out. His attempt is just a raspy breathless small gust of air. He just nods his head 'yes' as he continues to cough. "Of course you are, Michael. Your contact has been fulfilled. You must go and rest now. It won't be long before the next. You need your energy now." Seraphin says to him as she extends her arm gesturing at the door behind him.

Michael nods his head acknowledging that he understands her. He turns around and opens the door to the study. Seraphin walks around the table and exits into the hallway, where she waits for Michael to close the door and escort her to the main door. Michael stumbles out of the room and uses the hallway walls to stabilize himself as he escorts Seraphin to the front door. He unlocks the deadbolt and turns the handle. He stumbles back as he opens the door and sees the hallway is back where it is supposed to be. He gestures to Seraphin to exit the suite. Seraphin, with the same smile on her face, walks through the door and turns around to face Michael. "Thank you Michael. Get your rest. I will be back soon to go over our lessons." She says to Michael.

Michael just nods his head as he closes the door. He deadbolts it shut again and turns around. He stands there for a moment before he drops to the ground. He places his back against the door and spreads his legs on the floor. He reaches up to rub his neck. The slightest touch to his skin sends sharp pains through his neck. He drops his hands to his side and stares in front of him at the empty hallway. Michael's eyes begin to get heavy and he closes them. He sits there as he feels restlessness overcome his body. He feels tears start to form in his eyes again. He's too tired to cry or scream or anything. He musters up enough energy to force out three words to himself out loud.

"That's three."

ABOUT THE AUTHOR PAGE.

MICHAEL CLAYBOURN KNOWS WHAT IT'S like to be at arm's length with darkness. A storyteller at heart, Michael channels his struggles with mental health and intrusive thoughts into gripping fiction, creating evocative stories that don't just entertain but really resonate with his readers on a deeper level. His hope is that other readers who feel lost in their own darkness might find a flicker of light between these pages.

Living in a small town in Illinois, Michael is an adamant believer that creativity isn't confined to degrees or systematic study—it's born from life experience, struggle, and an inextinguishable desire to be. His stories never shy away from the darker side of life. Rather, they face it head-on, offering a mirror to anyone who has ever felt alone in their battles. Because no matter how deep the shadows stretch, there's always a reason to turn the page.

His debut novella, *S.O.L.O- Contract Three: Andrew Simmons*, is the outset of a thirteen-part series exploring the full spectrum of the human experience—raw, unfiltered, and painfully relatable. To connect with Michael and get updates on his latest releases, follow him on Instagram or TikTok.

If you, or someone you know is struggling with mental health. Please know, you are not alone. Help is available. I know first hand that mental health struggles feel isolating. You don't have to carry the weight of those emotions on your own. Help is available. If you need help, please don't hesitate to reach out to NAMI- National Alliance on Mental Illness at nami.org or dial 988 for immediate help.

www.ingramcontent.com/pod-product-compliance
Lightning Source LLC
Chambersburg PA
CBHW030009010826
48973CB00009B/2733